T0198581

UNSEEN SCARS

UNSEEN SCARS

JDB

UNSEEN SCARS

iUniverse books may be ordered through booksellers or by contacting:

iUniverse
1663 Liberty Drive
Bloomington, IN 47403
www.iuniverse.com
1-800-Authors (1-800-288-4677)

Because of the dynamic nature of the Internet, any web addresses or links contained in this book may have changed since publication and may no longer be valid. The views expressed in this work are solely those of the author and do not necessarily reflect the views of the publisher, and the publisher hereby disclaims any responsibility for them.

Any people depicted in stock imagery provided by Getty Images are models, and such images are being used for illustrative purposes only.
Certain stock imagery © Getty Images.

ISBN: 978-1-5320-9955-7 (sc)
ISBN: 978-1-5320-9956-4 (e)

Print information available on the last page.

iUniverse rev. date: 04/24/2020

Letter from the Author:
To all who read this story:

Thank you for taking the time to read my story. I did not put anything personal about myself in this book but there are pieces of real life events and experience that have been shared. I am a veteran myself and have seen how hard it is for some of my brothers to get over the things they have seen or done. I hope everyone enjoyed the story and understands that even people they have known their whole life may be in pain and just not showing it. Take the time to tell and show everyone how much they mean to you and show that you are there to support them if they ever need it.

Now to my fellow veterans and active service members. I hope those of you that read this book enjoyed it as well. Marines I am sorry there are not any pictures for you to follow along with, I will try to add some in my next story. j/k I know some of you can sound out the three letter words. Ok back to business. Yes, I put in some real info about the military and I know that some of it may not be 100% accurate. That was done on purpose so that no matter what unit or training you went to, I hoped that everyone could find a connection to the story.

I want to dedicate this book to Soldiers, Sailors, Marines, Airmen and Coast Guardsmen who fight their demons on their own.

I dedicate this book to everyone that struggles internally with problems that they need help with even if they do not ask for any.

This book is also dedicated to the ones that have lost that battle

Remember one thing. You are never alone and you do not have to fight on your own. Reach out and grab all the helping hands. They are there for you.

CHAPTER 1

FRIENDS

It was a hot Georgia summer in the late afternoon when a woman and her child pulled up to a local park for a little play time after a long and busy week. The heat had cooled down from the earlier afternoon temperatures and the sounds of birds chirping, with the buzz of cicadas filled the air. They were the only two at the park for the time being.

A small path led from the parking lot to one of the four playground sets that scattered the landscape of the park, with a walking trail that outlined the area. A recreational field was located towards the back of the property as well as restrooms and a water fountain. The lady called her son over to tell him where he should play so she wouldn't have to chase him all around.

She pointed to one of the playground sets that had a handful of things he could play on while she sat at a bench on the side of the path that wound its way around from playground to playground.

Johnny's mom had taken him to this park because it was just down the road from their new house. Johnny and his family had just moved to the area about a week ago and this was the first time they were able to relax after unpacking and setting up their new house, enrolling Johnny in school and all the other hassles that came with moving. Johnny's dad was at home finishing up his office, where he would work from time to time when not at the main office of a new branch for the law firm he worked for. The heads of his firm trusted him to head up the new branch due to his dedication and hard work. Johnny's mom sat on the bench and watched as he climbed up and down the monkey bars and going down the slides.

A woman approached with her son and asked Johnny's mom if she minded her sitting down next to her. "No, I don't mind... please have a seat." Johnny's mom replied. The lady thanked her and took her seat as her son ran off to the playground where Johnny was playing.

A little boy came up to Johnny and said, "Hi, I'm Billy." Johnny dropped off the balance beam and looked at the boy and replied, "Hi I'm Johnny, wanna play?" Billy shook his head and they both took off running around together playing on the seesaw and merry go round and the other playground equipment.

On the bench Billy's mother broke the awkward silence by introducing herself "Hi, I'm Jane, and that's my son Billy." Johnny's mother looked over at her with a smile "Hi, I'm Trish and my son is Johnny." The ladies started talking with Jane asking if they were new around the area. Trish explained to her that her husband just got promoted and was asked to move here to open a branch for the law firm Jude, Jim & Jackson. Which worked mostly with injury cases and other accident victims.

Trish asked how long they have lived in the area. Jane told her that they lived there ever since Billy was born. She went on to tell her that Billy's dad worked as a car mechanic in the day and picked up occasional side jobs to make extra cash during the night.

Jane commented on how well the two boys were playing together and asked how old Johnny was. "He turns 7 next month." Trish responded. "Ohh that's nice, Billy just turned 7 last weekend." Jane responded. The ladies conversed some more while the two boys played to their little hearts content.

As the sun started getting lower, Trish called Johnny over and told him it was time to head home for dinner. Johnny whined about not wanting to leave just then and wanted to play longer with his new friend. Trish just looked at him, smiled and said, "Don't worry we can come back again." She then held his hand as she led him back to the car. Johnny turned before getting in the car and yelled bye to his newfound friend.

Back at home Johnny told his dad about his new friend as they sat down for dinner. His dad sat there smiling as Johnny went on and on about this kid he met and how much fun he had playing with him.

Jane took Billy home where his dad was napping before having to go out to work one of his side jobs. Billy was excited about his new friend and wanted to tell his dad everything, but his mom told him to go play in his room quietly while she made dinner. Billy's dad awoke from his nap to the smell of pork frying in a pan. He checked his watch and realized he had to hurry and get ready for his next job. Billy heard his dad rustling around and got excited because he was now able to tell him about his new friend.

Billy hurried out of his room and down the short hall to see his dad putting a pork chop in his lunch pail and head for the door. "DAD! I want to tell you about my new friend," Billy exclaimed. His dad turned to him and said "I would love to hear about it, but I am running late. Maybe tomorrow you can tell me about him." Billy's head just sank as his father gave him a one-armed hug and headed out the door.

Jane stood in the doorway to the kitchen and watched as the exchange happened. As Billy turned towards the living room his mom called him over and told him to sit down for dinner. After Billy finished eating, he went into the living room and watched TV as his mom cleaned up. A short while later his mom instructed him to go shower and get ready for bed.

Night fell and Billy was asleep in his room, his mom was up watching tv in the living room waiting for her husband to get home. Around 11:30 the front door opened and her husband came strolling in. She greeted him in a stern but loving way. "What did I do wrong now?" he asked. She went on to tell him how distant he seemed towards their son that evening before he left. "All he wanted was to tell his father about his new friend and spend time with you." She scolded. He dropped his head and figured that she may have been right. She then told him to go clean up before he came to bed. After taking a shower he decided to make one more stop before going to their bedroom.

Billy's dad opened the door to Billy's room to find him in a deep sleep. He went in and sat down beside him and gently nudged Billy until he finally opened his eyes. "DAD!" he shouted. Billy sat up and hugged his dad. Billy's dad wrapped his arms around him and asked him to tell him about his new friend he met that afternoon.

CHAPTER 2

GROWING

Over the next few weeks of summer Johnny's mom took him to the park a few times each week where Johnny would go and play with Billy when he was there while she talked with Jane. The two boys would play together and every time it was different, sometimes they would be cowboys and Indians, other times they would pretend to be soldiers, or they would play hide and seek. Every day that they played was a different adventure for them. The mothers grew very close too, spending the day talking about what or how their husbands were doing. Gossip about other people from their neighborhoods and plan lady dates for them to go shopping or just get coffee.

Each day they spent together was time they cherished as it was a break from their housework, from their boys pestering them and a chance to just sit down and either enjoy a slight peaceful bliss or to talk and enjoy a grown-up conversation.

Summer came to an end and school started for both boys. Johnny was lucky as they both ended up in the same class. First grade was easy for them and went by pretty quickly as they were able to spend time together and help each other with their reading, writing and math lessons.

It would end up being two more years before they would be in the same class again. This wouldn't stop them from playing at recess or after school during those years as their closeness grew each year they did.

In the summer both boys would sign up for baseball and football in the fall and helped each other with learning the game and the position they played. They would spend the night at each other's houses before games and each mom took turns taking the boys to and from games and practice. Both the boy's parents would show up for the game itself, but this allowed the moms and dads to have some alone time.

By fifth grade the boys were as close as brothers. They weren't the most popular kids but weren't ones to be picked on either. This came to light one day around October when Johnny was in the cafeteria walking to get ice cream when a bigger kid from another class walked up behind him in the ice cream line and pushed him down. Other kids started making a commotion when out of nowhere Billy came flying in and landed a blow to the side of the bully's head. Johnny was not one to back down either. Just getting back to his feet he hurried over to the bully lying on the ground and jumped on top of him and began to punch him in the face repeatedly. Billy had to pull Johnny off the kid before the teacher came over and escorted the kids to the principal's office. All three received 1-week detention.

When the boy's moms showed up to pick them up from school, they were furious. Each got in their own cars where their moms proceeded to scold them. Once home the boys waited in their rooms while their mothers told their fathers, what happened.

Johnny's dad came to his room and asked for his side of the story. Johnny told him that he went to get ice cream and a kid behind him pushed him down. Then Billy knocked the kid down and that he got up and punched the kid for pushing him down. Johnny's dad sat and listened to his son's story.

Johnny finished and terror filled his eyes as he thought he was about to be spanked. His father stood up and looked at Johnny and said. "Son, I am a little mad at you, but I am also proud of you." Johnny looked confused as his father continued "It's ok to stand up to a bully. Just make sure you never are the bully. I won't punish you this time but remember one more thing, always try to find another option before resorting to violence." Johnny just looked at his father as he turned and left the room.

Billy was scared sitting on his bed thinking of running away or hiding, afraid of what his father was going to do. The door opened and Billy jumped back to the head of the bed. "Son, what happened." He demanded. So, Billy recounted what happened and watched as his father stared at the ground. After he finished his father just turned to the door and as he exited, he said "Good job." And then left his room.

At school the next day the boys were a little less enthusiastic then the previous day knowing they had to stay for detention. The week went by fast for the boys and the rest of that semester seemed to follow. Christmas break came and went.

The start of the next semester was in full swing before they knew it. The second half of the semester didn't go by any slower and without warning they were at the end of their middle school career.

With one month left to go the boys were excited for their summer break. "I can't believe next school year we will be in 9th grade" Johnny said. Billy shook his head in excitement. "Yeah it's going to be great" Billy responded.

CHAPTER 3

A TRAGEDY

Billy was counting down the days till the last day of school. "28 and counting" he said to his mom as he came running through the door after getting off the school bus. His mom just laughed and shook her head in agreement. "Hey Billy" she shouted. "Yeah" he yells from his room. "I need to run to the store to pick up some groceries, will you be ok by yourself for a few minutes?" she asks. "Yeah," he shouts again. Billy was changing his clothes so he could ride his bike and meet up with Johnny. Jane left the house and went off to the grocery store.

Billy was ready to go meet up with Johnny at a creek on the other side of town they found one day while out riding on an old hiking trail in a wooded area last summer.

Johnny was already there when Billy finally showed up. "Hey man what took so long?" Johnny asked. "Sorry man. My dad came home early not feeling well and I had to make him some soup before I could come." Billy responded. They both joked and played around in the creek and searched for crawdads. A few hours went by and it was time for both of them to head home for dinner.

They both rode together for a while till they came to the road where they would split off to their own houses. Johnny shouts "Alright see you tomorrow at school." Billy replies "Yeah see ya tomorrow." Johnny arrived home and greeted his parents and went to wash up for dinner.

As Billy approached his street, he saw a police car parked in front of his house. Scared Billy pedaled faster getting to his yard as fast as he could. His thoughts racing to his dad and hoped that his father wasn't that sick. He swung open the door to find his dad sitting in a chair with the police officer standing a few feet in front of him. Billy's alarm lessened seeing his father was awake. However, Billy's heart began to race as he noticed his father had been crying. "WHATS WRONG?" Billy shouts as he runs to his father. The officer looks down and says, "I'm sorry young man." But before the officer could finish Billy's dad grabbed him and held on to him. Now more concerned "What's wrong dad?" he asked in a worried voice. Beginning to look around the room, "Where's mom? Shouldn't she be back by now?" he began to question.

Billy's dad did his best to hold back the tears as he mustered the strength to tell Billy "Billy, your mother is gone. She won't be coming home anymore." Billy's eyes beginning to water "Where did she go?" He asked. In a crying voice his father responded, "She went to heaven." Billy began to cry shaking his head no. "No, she went to get groceries" he proclaimed. Billy's dad trying to pull himself together for his son "I know Billy, but on her way home another car side swiped her. She didn't make it" he says softly to his son. Billy begins to cry harder and buries his head into his dad's chest.

Meanwhile Johnny was at home getting ready for bed as his parents tucked him in. "Thank God it's Friday tomorrow" he says to his parents as they walk out of his room.

The next day Johnny's mom woke him up, packed his lunch and rushed him off to catch the school bus. After the morning rush calmed, Trish now had time to relax. She grabbed a cup of tea and turned on the tv to the morning news. *"Yesterday evening a drunk driver ran a stop light and crashed into another car. The driver of the second vehicle died at the scene."* The news reporter continued on with the story as Trish just thought to herself how tragic. When suddenly the reporter says, *"The name of the deceased driver is Jane Derst, she was a mother of one."* Trish jumped from her seat and ran to the door looking down the street to see if Johnny was still at the bus stop. She could still see his red backpack as she ties her robe up and sprints out the door calling for Johnny.

Johnny hears his mom calling him and turns to see her running down the sidewalk. Johnny looks on confused and half amused by the site of his mom running. He starts walking towards her with a smirk. "What is it mom?" he said as she approached him. "Come back home now. I will drop you off later, but you need to come home now." She proclaimed. Johnny, now a little frightened, followed his mom back home. "What is it mom?" he asked again more timidly. "I will tell you when we get inside. Trish and Johnny went back to the house and Trish sits Johnny down on the couch. "Now Johnny, I need to tell you something very important, ok?" she said, Johnny looked more frighten now, "OK mom" he says shaking. "Billy's mom…." She paused. "Billy's mom was killed in a car accident last night." She continues as she grabs a hold of her son and hugs him.

Johnny's heart breaks for his friend and tears roll down his face. "Is Billy ok?" he asks not knowing what or how it happened. Trish still holding him tells him, "I will call Billy's dad and see if there is anything we can do."

Johnny didn't go to school that day as Trish decided to make dinner for Billy and his dad. She called her husband and informed him on what happened as well. He left work early and headed home to help her with prepping the food and watching after Johnny who just sat around feeling hopeless.

The next few days were tough for Billy and his father. He was glad to see Johnny each day even if it was just for a short time when his family brought over food for them to eat. Billy's appetite really wasn't there. Billy's dad greatly appreciated the gesture, but he felt lost and didn't really know how to show his gratitude at the time.

The day of the funeral finally came, and Billy sat in the front row with his dad and grandparents. They cried as the preacher read off his mother's life story, from her birth, to meeting his father, then to her happiest moment, Billy's birth. Johnny sat a few rows back with his parents and watched with tears in his eyes as his friend said goodbye to his mother.

After the service everyone followed in their car to the burial site and gathered around as a few more words were spoken before they lowered Billy's mom into the ground. Johnny walked up to Billy and gave him a hug and told him how very sad he was for Billy and that he would do whatever he could to help his friend. Billy just cried trying to wipe away his tears and thanked his friend.

After a few moments Johnny had to go, he told Billy he would see him when he came back to school. He waved bye to his friend as he walked to his family's car.

Billy stood with his father as the rest of the guests began to leave. Both were lost, confused, and unsure of what to do now. Jane was the glue that held them all together. She made sure Billy was ready for the day, made sure he was fed, and cared for him when he was hurt. For her husband, Jane was the comfort for him after a hard day and a few hard nights of work, his moral compass and his reason for everything he did. With her gone now, they were lost in a maze of emotions.

Billy's grandparents were waiting by their car for Billy and his father to join them so they could take them back home. His grandparents watched as Billy and his dad finally found the courage to walk away from her grave and make their way back to what now seemed like an empty house.

CHAPTER 4

A LONELY SUMMER

The next school day Johnny was waiting for Billy at the entrance to his classroom, wanting to check on him and make sure he was ok. The bell rang and still no sign of Billy. Johnny didn't think much of it, thinking that he may be a little late especially due to current events that had taken place.

Johnny ran to his classroom and made it just before the second bell rang. Johnny sat in class and watched the time tick away. "When the bell rings at the end of class I will go see Billy then," he thought to himself. The minute hand finally made it around to the hour mark and the bell rang, Johnny jumped up and ran out the door. When he got to Billy's class, he looked around to see if he was there but still no sign of Billy.

Johnny went on the rest of the day looking for Billy, but he never showed up. Johnny figured he may have taken an extra day off school, so he decided he would call him when he got home.

School finally let out and Johnny hurried to the bus. As soon as the bus let him off, he ran home. Johnny threw his bookbag down and ran straight for the phone. The line rang and rang and rang, but nobody answered. Johnny figured he would try again later.

Johnny did his homework and watched tv while his mom started making dinner. His father came home and asked how his day was and talked to him about general things until Trish called them all for dinner. They all sat at the table, ate their dinner and discussed their day. When Johnny finished his plate, he excused himself from the table and went to call Billy. The phone rang again and still no answer. Johnny was growing a little concerned, so he told his mom and asked if they could go over to his house. Trish looked at Johnny and told him that they would go over after school on Friday if he didn't show up by then. Johnny didn't want to wait two more days but agreed to his mom's terms and went to his room to try and distract himself from his thoughts of his friend.

The two days came and went, Johnny was anxious about going to see his friend that day. When Johnny got home after school, he changed his clothes and told his mom he was ready to go. She stopped what she was doing and ushered him to the car.

They drove over to Billy's house, but when they got there nobody was home. No lights were on nor any cars in the driveway. The house appeared deserted. They knocked on the door just to make sure and when nobody answered Johnny became sad, not knowing what happened to his friend. He got back in the car and they drove back home.

The rest of the month went by and school was finally out, Billy never showed up to school for the remaining days and no one had heard anything other than his mother had died.

Summer started and Johnny didn't know what he wanted to do. He had planned to hang out with Billy all summer and do all the things he was accustomed of doing with him. With no idea where Billy was or when he was coming back or even if he was coming back, Johnny didn't know what to do.

During the early part of summer Johnny tried to play baseball but it wasn't the same without Billy. He ended up quitting a few games into the season and decided that he would stay at home. However, after a few days at home Johnny was becoming bored and anxious. He started going to the creek and other places that he frequently visited with Billy, but even that was mundane to him.

Halfway through summer Johnny's parents talked about what they could do for Johnny to try and get him out of the funk he was in. After discussing their options, they determined that it was time to go on their annual family vacation and hoped that it would help Johnny feel better.

Johnny's dad planned a trip to Key West for the three of them in a beachside hotel. Johnny's mom started packing their bags while Johnny was out riding his bike.

When he returned home late in the afternoon, he found his suitcase packed along with his mom and dads. "Hey what's going on?" he shouts. "Ohh hey sweetie. Glad your home, we have something to tell you." His mom replied. Johnny walks into the kitchen where his mom was finishing up dinner. "What's up mom?" he asks again. "Sit down honey and wait for your father." She replies. Johnny sits at the table while his mom places the dishes out, wondering what could be going on. He knew it was a trip of some sort but where to, and for how long.

Johnny's dad came strolling into the kitchen and greeted everyone. "Hello family." He said. Johnny still wanting to know what was going on. "OK, dad is here, now what's going on?" he demanded. Johnny's dad looked over at his wife, then back at Johnny "Well son. Tomorrow we are going on a vacation. We are flying down to Key West." Johnny just looked puzzled "But we normally go on vacation at the end of summer." He questioned. "We know honey, but you have been down ever since your friend left and we wanted to go early so you wouldn't be moping around the house all summer." His mom says. Johnny felt slightly upset at his parents, feeling as if they didn't understand how he was feeling or what he was going through. However, he was also a little happy to finally get out of his town and house for a short time.

The next morning, they all woke up, got dressed, ate breakfast and then headed to the airport. They dropped their bags off at the ticket counter and made their way through security. They sat at their designated gate for about 2 hours before boarding began. Shortly after boarding they were in the air and off to Key West.

They spent a week on vacation at a nice ocean front hotel in a room that overlooked the white sand beach and clear blue waters. Johnny found a slight reprieve from his loneliness while playing in the ocean and hotel pool as well as going out to eat and meeting new people. The sun, sand, and the sounds of the crashing waves were enough to distract him from the lonely feeling he had when he was at home.

Once they returned home he was able to fight off the feeling for a few days before he found himself back where he was before they left. He tried calling his friend again hoping that maybe while he was gone his best friend came back but still no one answered the phone.

Johnny spent the rest of the summer trying to find things to do to distract him from missing Billy, but to no avail. Everything he did was a temporary bandage that would constantly fall off. There were a few days he was able to distract himself more from his thoughts as it neared the beginning of school but not enough to overcome his feeling of being alone.

CHAPTER 5

REUNION

It was the last day of summer break, Johnny for the most part was ready for school. He was nervous about going to school for the first time without his best friend even though he had other friends in school. None were as close as Billy was to him. He actually felt nervous for his first day of school the same way he did when he first moved to the area and started school.

That night Johnny laid out all his clothes and put his backpack out by the front door. In the morning Johnny was going to be a high schooler and he wanted to make sure he was ready.

The next morning Johnny was waiting at the bus stop eager to see who he was going to be in class with. The bus pulled up and Johnny got on greeting a few of the other kids he knew and took his seat near the back of the bus.

Johnny arrived at school and made his way to his homeroom class. The teacher greeted each student as they entered and made their way to their seats. Every seat had an empty name plate on it for the students to fill out indicating that every seat should be taken, but as the final morning bell rang there was still one empty seat. Johnny looked around and wondered if that person was running late or if anyone else had any idea of who was supposed to be sitting there.

The teacher, Ms. Johansson was just starting roll call and was on the second name when the classroom door slowly opened. Johnny and the rest of the class turned their heads as another student entered the room. "BILLY!" Johnny shouts. Billy's head turns towards the voice to see Johnny smiling from ear to ear. "Hey Johnny." Billy says. Ms. Johansson looking sternly at the two of them "Uhh Hmm…. Are you going to take your seat?" She says sternly. Billy made his way to the empty seat and placed his bag on the ground as the teacher continued her roll call. After she makes her way through her list, she begins to pass out paperwork for the students to go over and sign.

As everyone is going over the paperwork Johnny tries to get Billy's attention to find out what happened to him. *"Billy… psst… Billy."* Johnny whispers. Billy looks over at Johnny and mouths the word "what." The two of them have a silent conversation in which Billy tells him they will talk about it at lunch when they have more time.

Class ended, Billy and Johnny were able to get together for a few minutes before their next class started. Billy didn't say much except he was happy to see Johnny again.

The next two classes for them were in separate rooms. Billy tells Johnny he will see him at lunch as they both go to their next class.

Lunch time rolls around and Johnny hurries to the cafeteria to meet up with Billy to find out what happened to him. Billy arrived shortly after Johnny; both get in line for lunch. "What happened to you?" Johnny asks, Billy just shrugs his shoulders and says, "My dad sent me to live with my grandparents for the summer." Johnny questioned Billy wondering why his dad did that, Billy explains what happened while they sat down to eat. "My dad was depressed and didn't want to deal with trying to raise me and find a way to get over my mom's death. So, he sent me to live with my grandparents for a while so he could figure everything out. It turned into all summer when it was only supposed to be a few days to maybe a week or two." "Ohh, man I'm so sorry. That must have been hard for you." Johnny responds. "At first it was, Dad didn't call or anything the whole time I was there which was what made it so hard, but I understood why… I think. The other thing that really sucked was not being able to hang out with you. There aren't many kids that live where they do so I just sat around the house most of the time." Billy continued. Johnny shakes his head and agrees and then asks, "So your dad finally came and got you?" "Not exactly, my grandparents are not my legal guardians so they would not have been able to put me in school and this school is way too far for them. So, they called my dad and told him that they were bringing me back for school." Johnny just looked on before asking "How is your dad?" Billy turned away not wanting to answer.

The lunch bell rang and saved Billy from Johnny's question. The boys got up and headed to their next class which they had together. Johnny didn't push the issue of Billy's dad and just talked about what each one of them did for the summer.

The rest of the school day went by relatively quickly and before they knew it the end of the day bell was ringing. Johnny met up with Billy by the busses and made plans to hang out later.

Once Johnny got home he hurried and finished his homework, then raced down the stairs and shouted to his mom that he was going to the park and out the door he went. Johnny's mom didn't even have time to respond before he was out the door. She was happy to hear the excitement back in his voice and only wondered what it could have been that caused it.

Johnny was excited to tell his mom that Billy was back but figured he would tell her and his dad at dinner time.

The wind raced across Johnny's face as he pedaled as fast as he could to the park to meet up with Billy. Johnny arrived to find Billy waiting on his bike by the teeter-totters. Billy greeted him with a smile and both of them rode their bikes around the walking trails and talked, catching up even more on all the things they did while they were separated and how bored they were the whole summer. Time seemed to fly for the two, Johnny's watch indicated that it was time to head home for dinner even though it had been two hours, it only felt like ten minutes.

Johnny bid farewell to Billy and headed back home. Billy on the other hand hung around the park a little longer. Thoughts racing through his head in an avoidance of what was truly going on with him and wondering to himself if he should tell Johnny.

Billy didn't want to tell Johnny what was going on with his dad, thinking that it would just cause Johnny to worry or maybe even think differently of him.

A few weeks of school went by and Johnny and Billy were getting back to the way things used to be.

That changed one day when Billy showed up to school wearing long sleeves and pants when the weather was still hot outside. Neither one of them knew how things were going to go but this day would be the beginning of many more changes to come.

Johnny ran up to Billy to tell him some exciting news that he heard that morning. "Billy, guess what!" he asked as he slaps Billy on the shoulder excitedly. Billy flinches with pain but did his best to mask it and asks what it was that Johnny had to tell him. Johnny didn't really pay attention or notice the flinch and went on to tell Billy "Dude, I am gonna be a big brother." Billy smiles and says that's great as he makes his way over to his seat. Johnny goes to his seat and gets ready for the start of the school day.

The rest of the day went by and the two of them went on as normal. The end of the day came and while Johnny was talking to Billy out by the busses, he noticed that Billy would flinch in pain every so often, when the bookbag strap would slip further down onto his shoulder. Johnny asked if Billy was ok as he watched him carefully adjust the backpack up on to his shoulder. Billy nodded and told Johnny that he would meet up after he gets home. Johnny said ok and headed to his bus.

Johnny went to the park and waited for Billy after he finished his schoolwork, but Billy never showed. He went back home assuming Billy got caught with homework or possibly helping his dad with chores or something like that. Johnny hung around the house bored until dinner was ready. His mom and dad asked what he thought the baby would be and if he liked any names for it as well.

The next day at school Billy was absent, Johnny didn't really think much of it and thought that maybe he was sick. Seeing how the day before he didn't seem well and looked as if something was bothering him.

The next day Billy was back at school and Johnny asked how he was feeling, Billy just mumbled "yeah I'm good" Johnny looked hesitant at his answer. Something just didn't seem right about Billy and he wasn't acting like his usual self.

Johnny's suspicions grew over the course of the next two weeks as Billy would seem almost back to normal one day and on other days he was more standoffish. Johnny knew there was something more going on but didn't know what it was. Johnny became really concerned when a day came and Billy walked into school wearing sunglasses.

CHAPTER 6

HARD TIMES AND GOOD FRIEND

Johnny had noticed that Billy didn't remove the sunglasses the entire time in class and wore them as he went off to his next class. When they met up later in the day, he was still wearing them. Johnny tried to figure out why he was wearing them, but Billy was in one of his standoffish moods and it would be of no use trying to get anything out of him.

When Johnny got home after school that day, he asked his mom if he could talk to her. Trish could see that something was bothering Johnny and told him of course they could talk. She put down the duster she was using and sat on the couch and signaled for Johnny to come and sit beside her.

Johnny sat down and fiddled with his hands as he tried to find the words for what he wanted to say "Mom… I'm conc…. I'm worr…. I think something is wrong with Billy," he finally said. "Why do you say that honey" she asked. Johnny then proceeded to tell her about Billy wearing sunglasses that day and how he was acting, then told tell her about all the other times he acted off from his normal self and how he looked like he was in pain occasionally. Johnny's mom listened and put things together in her head, she had a bad feeling growing in her stomach as she feared her new suspicions were all but confirmed. She maintained a straight face so she wouldn't alarm Johnny to her thoughts and fears.

After he was done telling her everything his mom just looked at him and patted him on the back and said, "Well all you can do is just be there for him when he needs you" Johnny nods and heads to his room to play until dinner was ready

When Johnny's dad arrived home that evening Trish told him they needed to talk after Johnny goes to bed. When he tried to ask what about, Johnny came running into the room to greet his dad and got ready for dinner. Dinner was mostly quiet as Johnny's dad was still wondering what Trish needed to talk to him about. Johnny sat there contemplating if he did the right thing by telling his mom what he noticed or if he should have ignored it since Billy didn't say anything to him.

Johnny went off to bed that evening while his mom and dad stayed downstairs to start their conversation. Trish recounted everything that Johnny had told her before voicing her own concerns to him. He listened to every word and could tell that she was upset by the things that Johnny had told her. He then told her that tomorrow she needed to call the school and tell them they needed to check Billy for any injuries due to suspicious bruises she saw. He then told her that he would stop by Billy's house and talk with Billy's dad and see if there is anything going on that shouldn't be.

She asked if that was a good idea to which he replied that he just wanted to check on everything and wouldn't do anything to get into trouble and would leave if he felt things became hostile. She shrugged and then headed off to bed.

The next morning Johnny woke up and got ready for school, his mom packed his lunch and told him that she would drop him off today. Johnny looked puzzled but didn't think too much about it at first before wondering if he was going to be in trouble.

Johnny and his mom arrived at the school but instead of dropping him off she pulled into a visitor parking spot. "Hey mom, what's up?" He asked. "Ohh, nothing honey. I just need to speak with the principal." She replied. Shocked, Johnny asks, "Am I in trouble?" Johnny's mom was quick to tell him no and that it had nothing to do with him.

Back at home Johnny's dad was just leaving the house to make his way over to Billy's house hoping in the back of his mind that his wife's concerns weren't true and that everything was a big misunderstanding.

He arrived at Billy's house and made his way to the door and was about to knock when he heard a slight commotion from inside. He listened for a second to see if he could tell what was going on when the sound of something breaking caught his attention causing him to knock hurriedly on the door.

A few seconds passed and Billy's dad Samuel opens the door "Hi Dean. How can I help you?" Sam asks. The smell of whiskey, stale cigarettes and unbathed stench filled the air. In one of Sam's hands Dean notices a belt being gripped. "Hey Sam. I came to check on you." Dean finally responds. Sam stands blocking the entrance to his house looking at Dean. He then turns his head toward the house and yells "Hurry up boy. You're going to be late for school." Billy comes walking out of the back with his head down and squeezes out the door between the two men. Dean watches as Billy makes his way up to the bus stop as the bus approaches. Dean turns back to Sam, "May I come in?" he asks. Sam shrugs and moves away from the door and leads him into the living room. When Dean entered the smell almost became overpowering.

After Jane's death Sam became emotionally unstable and refused to come to terms with reality. He sent Billy off with his grandparents and went looking for solace anywhere he could. He thought he found it at the bottom of a bottle at a bar outside of town and spent the next few days hovering around the place before the bartender kicked him out. He slowly found his way back to work to make whatever he could in order to buy his liquid solace at his leisure. That didn't last long as he was fired for being drunk on the job.

Jane's life insurance check came and was more than enough to keep him in his drunken stupor for a short time. He ended up selling both of the cars he had to ensure the mortgage would be paid after he ran through the life insurance money.

His routine was disrupted when Billy ended up back at the house. His grandparents never made their way inside and had no idea of how bad off Sam really was.

Sam stood there in his boxers, shirtless with a pack of cigarettes that appeared to have bested him while trying to get one out to smoke. "So, what do you want to check up on?" Sam asks. "Well my wife has some concerns about Billy." Dean says. "Yeah and?" Sam replies. "Well my son came home and said that Billy looked like he was roughed up, like maybe he got into a fight." Dean continues. Sam finally gets a cigarette out and lights it as he replies back "What of it?" Dean looking around the room "Well I just wanted to come and make sure everything was ok here. Make sure it wasn't happening at home." Dean says, now feeling aggravated by the appearance as beer cans and empty whiskey bottles littered the room. "Well are you hitting Billy?" Dean asks outright, no longer willing to beat around the bush.

Sam exhales and says, "Did he say that." Sam getting angered continues "I told that boy he better keep his mouth shut" Dean now clearly upset responds "He didn't say anything, my boy noticed he wasn't acting normal and brought it to our attention." Sam not liking the tone that Dean was starting to use says "I may have knocked him around a little here and there but nothing the boy can't take." Dean snaps and before Sam could react, Dean slams his fist into his face sending a loud crack to echo through Sam's head.

Sam stumbles back as blood starts to pour from his nose. Dean charges forward and hits him again, this time his fist lands on Sam's forehead sending Sam to the floor. Dean grabs Sam and picks him up "How does it feel getting knocked around." Dean spouts off as he hits him in the stomach. Sam fell back again and the urge to vomit rumbled as Dean stood above him debating on hitting him again.

Meanwhile at school, Billy's bus pulls up to the school and as he gets off he is met by the principal. "Billy. Can you please come with me?" the principal asked. Billy shakes his head and follows the principal to the nurse's office where the nurse and the school resource officer are waiting. The nurse closes the door and turns to Billy. "Can you please remove your shirt," she asks. Billy looks around trying to figure out what is going on. "It's ok young man. Just remove your shirt" the officer asks. Billy slowly places his bookbag down and begins to remove his shirt. He gets the shirt halfway up his torso when the officer sees the bruises and quickly turns towards the door as he gets on his radio.

Back at Billy's house Dean is seen dragging an unconscious Sam out into the yard. He then walks over to the hose and turns on the water. Sam jerks awake suddenly by the cold water as it hits his face causing him to cough and stutter. "H...Hey...HEY... Cut it OUT" Sam says. Dean turns off the water and walks over to Sam and hands him a frozen chicken breast wrapped in plastic. "You don't have any peas or vegetables frozen so use this for now," Dean says as he crouches down beside Sam.

A few moments later a police car arrives with lights flashing, the officer gets out of the car and approaches the two men "Which one of you is Sam Derst?" he demands. Sam raises his hand and the officer approaches him and grabs the risen hand and twists it around Sam's back. "You're under arrest for child endangerment." The officer picks Sam up off the ground as another police officer arrives. The first officer leads Sam to his car as the second officer approaches Dean. "Hello sir. How are you?" He asks. "I am good officer; how may I help you?" Dean responds. The Officer looks over at the other car and asks, "What is your purpose for being here?" Dean looked around and said "My son is the one noticing something wasn't right with his friend. So, I came over to see if everything was ok while my wife informed the school." The officer wrote down notes in a notepad he had pulled from his belt as Dean was talking. "OK sir, may I ask. Do you know how Mr. Derst ended up like that?" Dean's head fell looking towards the ground. "Well he had admitted to hitting his son, I guess I snapped a little bit." Dean responded. "OK sir, I will have to take you in for assault." The officer said. Dean nodded, turned and placed his hands behind his back for the officer. Dean was cuffed and placed in the back of the other car.

A short time later both Dean and Sam were sitting in a holding cell when Sam approached Dean. "Hey Dean…." He paused. The courage to say what he needed to say escaped him. The feeling of being vulnerable was staggering and hard.

Sam had spent the entire car ride to the station contemplating his current life choices and wondered how he got so far down the road he was on. The thoughts of Jane filled his mind and he knew that if she saw him and the way he was today, she would have beat him senseless and left him. Better yet he thought, she would have killed him for the way he treated Billy. When he arrived at the station and placed in the holding cell he sat alone in the corner arguing with himself about what he needed to do.

Dean could see Sam was struggling. "Hey man. It's ok. Let it out." Dean says. Sam breaks down and begins to cry a little as he says "I need help. I don't know what happened to me?" Dean places a hand on Sam's shoulder and reaffirms him "It will be ok. You can get past this. It's just going to take time."

Sam and Dean sat in their cell for a few hours, when an officer walked up and called "Mr. Lang?" Dean stood up and acknowledged the officer. "You made bail." The officer said as he opened the door. Dean turned to Sam, "If you want, I will help you. However, you will have to do exactly what I say." Sam nodded and watched as Dean left.

When Dean walked out to the lobby, he found his wife waiting for him, "Hey honey," he said. She glared at him for a moment then gave him a small smile. "I talked with the school, Child services and Billy's grandparents, we all agreed to let Billy stay with us for the time being." Dean shook his head in and turned to leave. "Now let's get you home before the boys get there."

Billy rode the bus with Johnny after school and was greeted by Trish at the bus stop when they got off. "Hey boys." She said. "Hey mom." Hey Mrs. Lang." they responded. Trish walked them both home and informed them that after dinner they would take Billy to his house so he could gather his things to bring back to their house.

Everything went smoothly and for the next few days everything seemed to be going well for Billy.

Billy was slightly mad at Johnny and his parents for everything that happened to his dad but also was appreciative at how much they cared for and were helping him and his father.

Billy was also upset with his dad for beating him and everything else that he did and what he turned into but at the same time it was his dad and he still loved him and wanted him to come back home. As time went on Billy slowly grew accustomed to living with Johnny and his family.

CHAPTER 7

TIME GOES ON

Dean offered to represent Sam in his case if he agreed to all of his terms and sought the help he needed, Sam accepted Dean's help. A few weeks had passed before his case was brought before a judge. His hearing was brief, the prosecutor and Dean made a plea deal in which Sam would plead guilty, his time served would count towards his total time issued by the judge, he would enter rehabilitation and seek counseling and would have supervised visitation with his son if Billy chose to visit during this time period. Sam also agreed to have the charges against Dean dropped as well. The Judge agreed with their deal and ordered an 8-month jail sentence, after time served was calculated he would end up with a little over 6 months locked up. Sam was happy with his sentence and thanked the Judge and Dean before he was taken by the deputies. Billy did not show for his father's court date because he didn't want to see his father be handcuffed and taken away.

Billy did go see his dad a few times while in jail, most of which were for the holidays. Billy missed his dad and wished things could go back to the way they were before his mom died. It always hurt whenever he would visit, seeing his father in a prison uniform and unable to get too close due to the rules the court had in place. Through all of this he did have Johnny and his family to fall back on. He was very grateful to Johnny's parents because they made the time for him to go visit his father even as Trish got further into her pregnancy.

Life at the Lang house was getting more and more interesting. Johnny and Billy were practically real brothers after a few months of living together, even more so than before when they were just close friends that acted like brothers. Billy had grown used to the Lang's and found the family he had been missing since the death of his mother and incarceration of his father.

Soon a little girl blessed the house as Johnny's little sister was born, both boys felt proud to be big brothers and did everything they could to help out with his new sister Lilly during the first few weeks after she came home. The first few months proved tiring as the baby would wake up crying every few hours. The two boys would wake every time they heard her and when she quieted down they would try to get back to sleep. When it seemed like they were on the brink of going back to sleep the baby would cry again.

School finally came to an end and Billy would go stay with his grandparents for a few weeks. They apologized almost every day he was there for not being there and protecting him from the abuse he received. Billy wasn't mad at them but he did enjoy being spoiled as they tried to make up for it by being over affectionate and buy him things he really didn't need.

Billy returned to the Lang's in time for the family vacation, seeing as Billy was now part of the family Johnny and his parents didn't think it right to go without Billy.

Billy would also go visit his dad who was still in rehab and counseling after finishing his six-month stint in jail. He was still upset by everything but was at least attempting to keep his father in his life.

Once Sam finished his jail sentence a friend from his previous job offered him a room to stay in while he completed rehab and got counseling. Sam still had to be under supervision when his son visited and could only do so at his rehab or counselor's office.

Johnny and Billy started to get deeper into the life altering changes of puberty and things were starting to take a turn for the boys who started finding other things that piqued their interest. Cars, girls, and of course alone time were the top of their new interests. The changes that were taking place were noticeable to Trish and Dean and they both started discussing when it would be the appropriate time for them to have the talk with the boys.

Over the course of their sophomore year Johnny's parents saw their attitudes change and how their concentration seemed to change focus and figured that now was the time to sit them down and go over the birds and the bees with them. Dean didn't want to overstep Sam if he wanted to be the one to give his son the Talk and informed Sam about the changes. Dean asked Sam if he wanted to have that discussion with Billy or would he be ok with Dean giving Billy the "TALK" along with Johnny. Sam was mad at himself because he knew it would be best for Dean to do it, and it got under his skin that he was in no position to talk to his son about those matters and didn't feel it was right to subject Billy to that type of embarrassment especially when there had to be a stranger in the room the whole time. Sam told Dean that he didn't mind if he did it and asked if he would make sure to let Billy know that if he had any additional questions he could always come to him if he wanted. Dean agreed and asked if there was anything else he would like for him to tell Billy before he left.

A few days later Dean sat both boys down during the spring break and decided to give them the "TALK." Even though the school provided a sense of sex ed, it still missed the finer points, kids do not only care about the bad side, they also want to know more about the fun side.

Dean told the boys about the birds and the bees and recapped a little of what the schools taught. He then went into other details about how to treat the other person they're with and how not to be pressured because the first time is never all it seems to be. He could tell that while doing so both boys were feeling awkward about hearing Dean talk about women and how certain parts are used and what type of feelings they should expect.

Dean finished up his talk and left the room with a big smile on his face, both of the boys sat there trying to get the thoughts out of their head that he had placed there. When Dean saw Trish in the living room, she asked how it went and he just smirked and said, "Well I think they may be more nauseated by the fact I knew all that stuff, then they were by the STD presentation at school." She laughed and both of them went on about their day while the boys did everything they could to get those thoughts and images out of their heads.

Summer rolled around again, causing Billy to get excited. His dad finally finished with all his mandated court orders and would be free to live with Billy and without supervision. Billy thought that this would be great because he could go live with his dad and be a family again.

Dean still had his hesitations about how Sam was after everything and didn't want Billy to get his hopes up but also didn't want to ruin Billy's hopes. On the last day of Sam's counseling session Dean drove Billy to the building where Sam was finishing up his last session.

Dean pulled up to the building and told Billy they would wait outside for his dad so as not to disturb the other patients. Billy was as happy as a six year old on Christmas morning.

Billy stood by the hood of the car and watched every time the door opened and someone would come out. Billy finally saw his dad coming out from the building and ran over to him. Sam smiled and braced for the impact from his son who was charging at full speed. Billy threw his arms around his dad and gave him the biggest squeeze he could, Sam squeezed his son back and told him that he was so happy to be able to see him without worrying about supervision.

Billy without hesitation asked, "So this means I can live with you again?" Sam's face went blank for a second before responding with "We will have to discuss it. Right now, I need a word with

Dean." Billy looked perplexed at his dad and asked, "What's there to discuss?" Sam looked down at Billy who wasn't much shorter than him now and said, "Let me talk with Dean and we will discuss it after." Billy pulled away and looked at his dad as he walked towards Dean.

Dean saw Sam walking towards him and started walking to meet him half-way. "How are you doing?" Dean asked. "I'm doing good Dean." Sam replied. They shook hands and Sam continued "I want to thank you for everything you have done for me, and for taking care of Billy." Dean nodded and told him that there was no need to thank him. He just did what he knew was right. Sam still thanked him and then said, "I still have one favor to ask." Dean asks, "What is it?" Sam looks at Billy and says, "I wanted to know if you would continue to keep looking after Billy for me?" Billy yelled "What. NO. I want to live with you now dad." Sam turned and placed his hands upon Billy's shoulders and says, "Look son… I want nothing more than to do that and reconnect with you and be a full-time father…. but while I was going through counseling I learned that I am not capable at this moment to take care of you much less myself. I need to get my life back together and learn to take care of myself before I can take care of you." Billy's eyes teared up and he pulled from his father's grasp and ran to Dean's car and slump down by the back tire.

Dean looked over at Billy and then back to Sam and says, "No problem Sam… just make sure you're able to give Billy everything he needs as a father before you take on that responsibility." Sam nodded then walked over to Billy. "Hey son…. I don't want you to think I don't want anything to do with you…. it's just… it's just that I am not capable of taking care of you the way you need. I still want to see you, spend time with you, talk to you and be in your life. I just don't think I can be a full-time dad at this moment." Billy, still crying, refuses to look up at him as he stands there.

Dean gives them a few seconds before walking over and asks, "Sam would you like to go grab a bite to eat?" Sam declines and tells them that he has a job interview that he must go to and tells them that next time he would love to go get food. Sam then looks at Billy then back to Dean without saying a word, the look on his face was all Dean needed to see for him to understand what Sam was going to ask. Dean tells him "I will take care of him. Go to your interview and start getting yourself back together" Sam bids farewell and tells Billy he will see him again and turns to walk to another car that was idling a few spots away from them with another patient that had already offered to drop him off at his interview.

Dean talks Billy into getting in the car and drives them home. Dean tells Billy his dad isn't doing this because he doesn't love him, it is because he does love him and wants to be able to do what's best for the both of them. Billy was trying to dry his eyes so Johnny wouldn't see him that way when they got back home as he asks Dean "What will Johnny and Mrs. Lang say.?" Dean looks in the rearview mirror since Billy decided to get into the backseat when getting in the car and tells Billy not to worry that they will understand.

Billy eventually got over what his dad did, but it did take some time for him to start talking to his dad again while sorting through his own emotions.

Johnny would help Billy work through things when he needed it and gave him space when he wanted it. Johnny felt bad for Billy for not being able to get what he wanted, but he did enjoy having him around.

As their junior year approached, neither one of the boys could have been prepared for what the year was going to do to them. Things were going to change and life was going to be forever different.

CHAPTER 8

A GIRL AND TWO BOYS

Johnny and Billy were in the first quarter of their junior year when they met Maddy, a new girl to their school and one that caught both of their attention. Maddy just moved to the area during the summer and was new to the school. She had blonde highlights throughout her light brown hair. She was around 5'10 and athletic. Maddy was a cheerleader at her previous school and was trying out for her new school's cheer squad and was becoming the gossip of the school.

Johnny was in the same second and third period class with her and sat just a few chairs behind her in each class, needless to say, he liked the view. Billy had fourth and sixth period class with her and both Johnny and Billy shared lunch together with her. Neither one of them would sit at the same table as her but both would look on in admiration. Every once in a while, they would swear they caught her looking at them as well.

At first, they didn't pay much attention to her personally and only spoke to each other about her when they would say things like "Dude, did you see that skirt she was wearing?" or "Hey man guess what... She bumped into me when I was trying to leave the classroom. I think she did it on purpose" Both boys were shy and nervous about talking to her directly.

Then one day out of the blue Maddy walked up to Johnny and handed him an envelope. Johnny sat there dumbfounded and stuttered "H..H..HI. I'm Johnny" without skipping a beat, she responds "Hi, I'm Maddy and I am throwing a party at my house this Saturday and I wanted to invite you." Johnny, still in disbelief that the girl who he had but would never admit to having a huge crush on, was inviting him to a party at her house. "Yeah… Cool. Thanks", He says while thinking in the back of his mind "what is wrong with me." Maddy smiles and turns away and hands out a few more envelopes to more classmates. Johnny finally snapped out of his daydream and decided he would wait till after school to tell the good news Billy.

Billy was in fourth period and found a note and an envelope on his desk. The note read "Hi. I wanted to invite you to a party at my house this Saturday. Signed Maddy." Billy looked up and saw her sitting off to the opposite side of the classroom where she normally sat, smiled and daydreamt about her for the better part of the class. He hadn't told Johnny, but Billy was crushing on Maddy also. Billy decided he would tell Johnny about it after school let out.

When school let out Billy and Johnny met at the bus with glaring smiles on their faces. Excited, they both couldn't wait to tell each other:

Johnny: "Dude, you will not believe what happened."

Billy: "No man… You won't believe what happened."

Johnny: "I just got……"

Billy: "To Maddy's party."

Johnny: "Yeah, how did you…."

Billy: "Me too."

Johnny: "Great we can both go then."

Billy nodded his head as they got on the bus.

The whole ride home they talked nonstop about going to the party and about Maddy and what they should wear and how they should act to look cool. Then reality set in, Billy looks at Johnny and asks, "Do you think your parents will even let us go?" Johnny ponders for a minute then says, "Yeah I am sure they will." "OK, but who and what are we gonna drive?" Billy asks. Johnny looks around thinking, "We will work that out later. We still have two days."

Johnny and Billy had just received their driver's licenses that summer, but neither one of them actually owned a car. They would borrow Deans or Trish's car when they needed to go to the store or if they were told to go run errands for Dean and Trish. They never gave it much thought about going to parties or even going on dates and needing a car to get around. They didn't have jobs and the only money they received was from finishing chores.

They boys finally got home and rushed into the house. Lilly was running around in a diaper shouting and laughing when she sees them enter the house and stops in her tracks. Billy looks down at her and says "hi" as the smile on her face got bigger and Johnny held out his arms as she runs to him wanting him to pick her up. She talks to them in baby and both just play along like they understand exactly what she is saying before putting her back down and calling for Johnny's mom. Trish enters the room and asked what the boys wanted, they proceed to tell her about the party and asked if they could go. Trish thinks for a second and tells them that she will discuss it with Dean and let them know.

Dean came home that evening and looked a little rough from his day. "How was your day honey?" Trish asked. "Well I was hoping to be finished with litigations today, but the judge had to leave for an emergency, and we couldn't get a ruling. Then to top it off my client thinks they can get more now and wants to push for it." She told him she was sorry and that she would try to help him relax. She then mentioned that the boys were invited to a high school party and they needed to discuss it.

The two boys were outside playing with Lilly while Johnny's mom talked to Dean. "The boys asked me today about going to a party they were invited to on Saturday." Dean looked at her and said "And?" Trish sits down beside him "Well from the sounds of it, it's going to be an unchaperoned high school party." Dean looks at Trish not sure what she was implying, before it finally hit him

"Ohh… OK. Well what should we say?" He asked. "Trish thought for a second and told him that she wasn't too sure about letting them go, but at the same time they are juniors and things like this are going to keep coming up. Dean listens to his wife's concerns and finally speaks up. "Well we did have a lot of fun at those types of parties." He says winking at her, causing her to blush a little before continuing on "I think we should let them go. They can take my car and if anything happens, I will pick them up in your car." Trish agreed and walked to the door and called the boys in. Lilly waddled her way in first followed by the boys as Trish had them sit down and told them that they could go but they needed to speak to Dean first.

Excited both boys thanked her and rushed to talk to Dean, "Hey dad, thanks for letting us go." Johnny said with a smile. Dean smiled and informed them that there are some rules that they will have to abide by if they wanted to go to any future parties. Dean sat the boys down and went over everything with them and doubled down on how much trouble they would be in if they did not follow his rules. The boys agreed to everything and ran off to their room and waited for dinner.

Two days came and went, and it was finally Saturday. The card each one received had the time and address to the party. The boys spent all day planning on what they were going to do and wear. Johnny's mom and dad just sat around and laughed at them, telling Lilly that they were both goofy and making her laugh as they could be overheard talking to each other asking what looked better and if one should style their hair this way or that way.

About an hour before the party the boys decided that it was time to shower and change. They didn't want to shower too early and chance stinking later on at the party.

The boys each took their shower and got dressed. Johnny finished first and rushed downstairs to ask his dad for the keys to the car. "You remember what we talked about right?" Dean asks. "Yes dad. I remember." Johnny responds. Billy finally joined Johnny and they both asked Trish how they looked. She gave them a thumbs up and they set off for the party.

The drive to Maddy's house was about thirty minutes with red lights and weekend traffic. Once they arrived, they knocked on the door and waited for it to open. Both were anxious and ready for whatever was going to happen that night. There were already a few cars there and music was playing, so they knew they were not the first to show up and hoped that they dressed appropriately. Maddy opened the door and greeted them to her party, she told them that everything was set up in the backyard, then led them through the house. She told them she was so happy they could make it and hoped that they had a good time. They both looked at each other smirking, trying not to overdo it and embarrass themselves.

Around 9 o'clock the party was well under way, a few other guests brought beer that they either swiped from their parents or had an older friend or sibling buy for them. Maddy was making her rounds playing hostess when she spotted Billy and Johnny by the pool sipping on cups with beer in it, talking to one of the friends from class.

Both Johnny and Billy were doing their best to seem cool, they would sip the beer slowly and would almost gag at the taste. Neither one of them had ever drank beer before and didn't like the taste. They hid their disgusted look every time they took a sip so others wouldn't notice or say anything to them.

Maddy walked up to them hoping to be able to talk for a while "HEY guys." She shouted as she approached them with another brunette following behind her. "Hey Maddy. Great party." They all said. Maddy pulls the brunette up beside her "I want to introduce yall to my friend Brittany or Britt for short." They all greeted Britt and began to talk.

Britt was slightly shorter than Maddy but just as pretty. She had darker hair and slightly fuller lips. She was a cheerleader also but was already a part of the squad when she met Maddy. Britt already knew who Billy was as she had a few classes with him the year before even though he really never noticed her. She was quieter and more reserved when not cheering and focused on her grades as she was already planning for college.

Before they knew it, the time was 11:30 and Johnny and Billy had to get home. They thanked Maddy again and said their goodbyes and left.

On the way home Billy told Johnny that he wanted to ask out Maddy and wanted to know if he was ok with it. Johnny wasn't sure what to say. He wanted to say no, but he didn't want Billy to be mad and think he was being selfish. He thought about it for a few seconds and says "Sure man. Go ahead." Johnny then asks, "When are you gonna do it?" Billy thought about it and concluded that he didn't know. He didn't want to rush into it, but also didn't want to wait too long.

CHAPTER 9

A BROTHERLY DISAGREEMENT

Johnny and Billy started to hang out with Maddy and Britt more and more as the first half of the school year went on. Billy still hadn't asked Maddy out but was getting close to doing it. Britt was becoming more flirtatious with Billy, but he hadn't noticed which drove Britt crazy. Johnny was playing it safe with Maddy and Britt not wanting to cause any trouble between the group.

The group had become a pretty regular site around the school and even after school. Johnny and Billy would go watch them practice and even attended a few of the school's football games. Maddy and Britt have even met Johnny's parents and even hung out at his house a few times. Trish thought the girls were polite and kind and didn't mind them hanging out. Dean knew something was going to happen, just didn't know what it was or when it was going to happen.

Dean's concerns were about to come to light on a brisk November day, Billy had borrowed one of the cars and gone to see his dad during the holiday break for thanksgiving and Trish and Dean were grocery shopping with Lilly while Johnny stayed home and played a video game.

A knock at the door took Johnny by surprise as he wasn't expecting anyone and everyone that left had a key. He ran down to answer the door and when he opened the door, he saw Maddy standing there. "Hey Maddy." Johnny said. "Hey, can I come in?" Maddy says. Johnny looks around and says "Sure Maddy" as he moves out of the way allowing her to enter.

She looks around and then asks, "So what were you doing?" Johnny unknowing what was going on says "Oh, I was just playing a game online." Maddy looks at Johnny and asks if she could watch him play. Johnny being a guy, was oblivious of the tone that Maddy was using and was soon to be in for a surprise.

Maddy had talked to Billy on the phone and found out that Johnny was at home without Billy around. When she arrived, she noticed the other car was gone and hoped that Johnny wasn't gone as well. She wanted to take the opportunity to tell Johnny how she feels about him. She didn't expect him to be home alone but figured she would try her luck.

Johnny leads the way to his room and pulls a chair up next to his bed where he was sitting and playing for Maddy to sit on. Maddy discarded the chair and sat on the bed with Johnny while he starts to play again.

Maddy had a crush on Johnny and didn't want to say anything in front of Billy because she could tell that Billy liked her. She had a chance to tell Johnny that she liked him with Billy being gone but wasn't sure how she would let him know and hoped that Johnny would pick up on the hints that she was dropping.

Maddy started moving closer to Johnny as he played his game until she was side by side with him. Johnny was to focused on his game and didn't pay attention to her. Maddy decided to see if she could get him to talk to her "Hey, you're really good at this game." She said. Johnny without looking away thanked her but assured her that he was far from good. The lack of attention was beginning to annoy Maddy.

Johnny being the average teenage boy was oblivious of Maddy's intent and thought to himself "What is she doing? Can't she see that I am trying to beat the other people. Why is she being so weird?" he continued playing and tried his best to ignore Maddy's quirks.

She sat there and thought for a bit and decided she would place her hand on his leg. This caused Johnny to stir a little as he felt her hand resting on his leg just above his knee. He glanced down quickly then back up to his game, Maddy noticed his glance and started to smile. She began to rub her hand up his leg then back down, moving it closer and closer towards his thigh. Johnny started to shift around becoming nervous about what was happening. His heart rate was climbing and his mind began racing as he started losing focus on the game.

Maddy's hand finally reached his inner thigh, Johnny threw the controller down as Maddy's hand moved in closer to his crotch. Maddy was smiling as she watched Johnny squirm in confusion and when he turned to talk to her, she planted her lips on his before he could utter a word.

Johnny was so shocked by the sudden actions of Maddy, that he lost his train of thought. Passion was starting to flow through him as he couldn't help but continue kissing the girl he had a crush on. Johnny's hand begins to rub up and down Maddy's side as the two begin to embrace each other.

Both of them pulled each other in the throes of teenage passion down on Johnny's bed. Johnny propped himself up on the side of Maddy so he could face down to her, while she laid on her back with her arms wrapped around Johnny's neck. Johnny's right hand began to explore more of Maddy's body rubbing up and down her side.

Outside Dean's car pulls up and parks in the driveway just past Maddy's car. Excited that Maddy had come over Billy rushes into the house "Hey" He says at a light shout, but no response. Billy looked around the downstairs and found no sign of Maddy or Johnny or anybody else. He then remembered seeing that the other car was gone and thought maybe they all went off somewhere. Billy decided to go upstairs and relax for a little bit and wait for everyone to get back.

When he got to the top of the stairs, he heard a low noise coming from Johnny's room. Billy thought to himself "Damn Johnny forgot to turn off his game again. Guess I will do it for him." Billy opens Johnny's door and finds Johnny kissing Maddy with one hand sliding down her pants. "WHAT THE FUCK!" Billy shouts. Johnny quickly pulls his hand out and jumps up. "Billy, let me explain" he stammers, but Billy was deaf with anger. "How could you do this to me. You know I like her… You knew I was gonna ask her out." Billy says. Maddy gets up and buttons her pants back. As Billy starts walking towards Johnny, Maddy tries to tell him "I like your brother… I mean I like you too, just not the way I like him," but Billy paid no attention. Johnny knew what was about to happen and was trying to find a way out of it, but before he could Billy rears back and swings at Johnny.

Johnny attempts to move but is still caught by the punch as it skimmed across his cheek. "OK Billy. You hit me, now let it go." Johnny says, but Billy rears back again and swings. This time Johnny moves out of the way and pushes Billy away. Maddy becomes frightened and not knowing what to do hurries out of the room, then the house and out to her car where she speeds off back home fearful of what was happening and blaming herself.

Back in the room Billy turns back toward Johnny and charges him, tackling him to the ground. Johnny struggles with Billy as both trade blows with each other hitting shoulders and arms. Johnny was finally able to break away from Billy and get back to his feet, Billy stands up quickly and goes to punch Johnny again, this time connecting with his nose. Johnny stumbles back, placing his hands over his nose checking for blood. "That's enough Billy." Johnny says muffled, but Billy kept coming. Billy pulled his fist back again and Johnny took the opportunity and placed a quick jab on Billy's nose. A loud crack can be heard as Billy stumbles, this time with blood starting to drip from his nose. Billy charged Johnny again and again they tussled with each other.

Both of them were beginning to tire as it seemed like they were fighting for hours but it was only a few minutes. Billy dropped his hands and fell to the ground trying to catch his breath. Johnny watched as Billy started to contemplate everything and decided to sit down beside him. Johnny put a hand on Billy's back and told him to listen and let him explain. Billy remained quiet as Johnny informed him of everything that happened and let him know that he would never intentionally do anything to hurt him. Billy shook his head and told him that he knows but seeing him with the girl he liked just drove him mad. Johnny understood and held no ill will towards Billy and both decided to get some fresh air and see if Maddy was still around.

A short while later, Billy and Johnny were sitting on the front steps getting some fresh air when Dean and Trish pulled up. Dean saw Billy and Johnny and already knew what happened without having to ask. Trish on the other hand began to freak out when she saw them and rushed over demanding to know what happened. Johnny looked at Billy and said, "We were playing around, and we fell down the stairs." Billy nodded and Trish stood there looking at them angrily knowing that wasn't the truth. Trish turned to her husband and says, "Dean... Do you hear this!?. They said they fell down the stairs." Dean had just got Lilly out of the car and was currently grabbing groceries and replies "Well if that's what they said happened, then that's what happened." The two boys look at each other then back at Trish as she looks sternly at them and tells them she knows that's not what happened and will find out the truth as she storms inside. Dean comes walking up and stops, he doesn't even look down at them and asks, "You two work everything out?" Johnny looks at Billy then back at his dad and both reply with yes, Dean looks down and says, "Good, let's not have this happen again." Dean then walks inside as Lilly comes stumbling up and looks at both of them before saying "owwy" as she points at their faces and waddles through the door. Dean could be overheard telling Lilly that they were both just goofy and dumb boys.

The next school day both of them had the remains of black eyes, swollen lips and Billy a busted nose as they walked through the halls. Billy sees Maddy standing by their lockers and looks at Johnny and says, "Go for it… plus Britt is pretty hot herself so…" he nudges Johnny in the side and smirks, they both approach Maddy. Johnny explains everything to her and that neither one of them blame her, she is relieved that they are not mad at her and asks what do they do now. They walk to class trying to figure out what they should do and decide to discuss it more at lunch.

Johnny and Maddy start dating shortly after that incident and Billy asks Maddy if she would be willing to hook him up with Britt.

The school year goes on and the group continues as if nothing ever happened.

CHAPTER 10

THE FIRST TIME

Johnny had been dating Maddy for a while now and whenever he would get his allowance from completing his chores, he would take her on small dates that he could afford. Johnny's hormones were a driving factor in his choices for date locations. He would pick somewhere there were people at first to calm his nerves and then would try to plan somewhere a little less occupied by the end of the date in hopes of getting lucky.

Maddy could spot his advances at the start of the night and always found a way to tease him but never let him get too far. She enjoyed being the cat in this game of cat and mouse and watch Johnny bounce between her paws looking for any type of release.

He would occasionally get to third base when she was feeling nice but mostly kept him stranded on second with a playful grin. Johnny had no idea what she was doing and thought that he just had to become more outright in his action so she would know what he was looking for.

Maddy wasn't completely against it, she just enjoyed toying with him too much to stop. However, those days were coming to an end for the both of them. Maddy and Johnny both were in-experienced in the matters of a full-on sexual encounter. They had played around and experienced the lesser acts but neither ever went all the way. Maddy finally decided to go all the way with Johnny and even told

Britt about it. Britt was excited and wanted to know everything afterwards. She too along with Billy hadn't done anything that extensive yet and she was nervous to do so.

Johnny planned a date where they would go to get dinner at a diner and then head near Atlanta where he heard about a drive-in theater and then hopefully somewhere secluded. Maddy liked the idea of going to a drive-in because she had never been, and it looked like fun in the movies. She decided that this would be the date that she would finally go all the way with Johnny.

The Day came and Johnny borrowed his dad's car for his date. Dean's car was a Lincoln Continental he used mostly for work. A leather interior and plenty of room to relax. Maddy liked Dean's car as it was roomier than her Volkswagen Beetle.

Dinner was delightful and both ordered food that would take less of a toll on their breath knowing that there would at least be some making out that night. Johnny walked Maddy to the door of the car and opened it for her trying to win some brownie points.

Maddy smiled and thanked him while he closed the door for her. Maddy had decided to wear a knee length skirt knowing where the night was going to go and was trying to make it a least difficult as she could. Johnny got in and set off for the drive-in.

The sun began setting as they arrived and pulled in line to purchase their tickets. Each screen was a double feature and Johnny asked which two movies she wanted to see. Maddy pointed to what she wanted to watch. Screen three had a comedy followed by a horror movie. It was also the most secluded screen set off to the side from the other two. Johnny bought the tickets and they made their way to screen three. There were only a few cars there already and started pointing to spots asking where she would like to park. Maddy looked around and told him to park on the back row so they could see the screen a lot better than being up close. Johnny was dumbfounded as there was no parking close to the screen where you couldn't see it through your windshield but obliged her and parked on the back row. A small snack stand was a few yards away and a couple of row down from them. Johnny excused himself and went to get popcorn and two drinks for them.

The first movie started, and both sat back laughed as the movie played on, Maddy would turn and look at Johnny and watch him for a few seconds before focusing back on the movie.

When the first movie ended, Johnny asked her if she wanted to stretch her legs before the second movie started. Maddy took the opportunity to get out and stretch her legs. She then excused herself to the bathroom and headed toward the snack stand. Johnny stood outside the car and waited for her to return. When she returned Johnny went to open the door for her again, but she turned him away and climbed into the back seat. Johnny looked puzzled walked around the car and opened the other back door and poked his head inside and asked "Hey, why are you back here?" Maddy looked at Johnny and replied, "No center console back here so I can sit closer to you for the scary movie." Johnny nodded in belief that she was concerned about getting scared and wanted to be closer. Johnny climbed in the back with her as they both got comfortable waiting for the movie to start.

The opening credits began to scroll by and Maddy pushed herself closer to Johnny. As the movie started into the story Maddy began to make her move. She began to rub Johnny's leg with her hand and nibble on his ear. Johnny's heart rate skyrocketed as he became aroused and nervous at the same time. Maddy moved to kissing him as she rotated her body to make it easier.

Johnny had made out with her many times but for some reason this felt different. Johnny tried to move around and find a more comfortable position for both of them. After a few minutes Maddy whispered in Johnny's ear "Do you have protection?" Johnny pulled back and replied "Are you serious? You sure you want to do this here?" Maddy nodded yes and Johnny pulled out his wallet where he had been carrying around a condom since they started dating. Maddy laid back in the seat with her head resting on the door armrest. Both of them were breathing erratically and their hearts were racing.

A few minutes later Johnny was zipping his pants and asking Maddy if she was ok. It wasn't as either one had expected, and both were relieved that it was finally over. Maddy didn't want to talk about it at the moment and sat there watching the rest of the movie. Johnny took a handful of napkins and wrapped up the condom and took it to the trash can and threw it away.

The rest of the night went by in a stale air and both were unsure of what they should say or even do.

Johnny was dropping off Maddy when she finally spoke and told him that she did in fact have fun and couldn't wait for their next date. Johnny smiled and went home. Maddy immediately called Britt to tell her everything.

Johnny got home and found Billy watching tv alone downstairs where he decided to stand in front of the tv. "Dude, can you move" Billy says looking up at Johnny who at this point had a huge grin on his face. "what is it?" Billy asks, Johnny just nods and Billy sounding more excited "No, way…. Did you really?" Johnny just nodded again this time with a bigger smile when Billy says "Don't just stand there dude. Tell me. How was it?" Johnny sat on a cushion next to Billy and told him "Man, it was amazing. So, there we were in the back seat at the drive in and she starts rubbing on me and all and I was like whoa slow down but she couldn't keep her hands off me. So next thing you know we going at it and by time we were done the movie was over." Billy just smiled and told Johnny "Man you are so lucky. I can't wait for Britt to let me go all the way." The boys talked a little longer with Johnny exaggerating a little bit more every time told the story.

Billy was jealous of Johnny at first and couldn't wait until he got the chance to catch up to his friend. Billy wouldn't have to wait long, however. After Maddy had told Britt about how awkward it was at first and how it hurt a little at first then started to feel better just before Johnny had finished made Britt think about it more and decided that she would let Billy go all the way the weekend after he came back from visiting his dad.

Two weeks later Billy and Britt were on a date at a local bowling alley. Having fun and enjoying their playful competition when Britt told Billy that her parents weren't going to be home until late that night because her dad took her mom to a play in Atlanta. Billy thought "ohh that's cool" not picking up on her hints. Britt didn't want to waste time hinting around waiting for him to guess what she was getting at and just asked "Do you want to go to my place now? Or wait for my parents to get home?" Billy took a second before tearing off the bowling shoes and shouting at her as he hurried to the counter throwing the shoes on top "What is taking you so long?" Britt laughed as she followed over and turned her shoes in and paid for the games they played and headed out to her car and drove them to her house.

Once at her house She led Billy to her bedroom where she sat him down on the bed and began kissing him. Just like with Johnny and Maddy both of their heart rates were racing, and Billy's hands were shaking a little from his nerves. Britt's thoughts were racing as she thought about what Maddy had told her what her first time was like. Billy could tell that Britt was nervous as much as he was and assured her that if she wasn't ready that he could wait. Britt shook her head and told him that she was ready now, but it was her first time and wasn't sure how it would be. Billy told her that it was his first too so they could take it slow. Britt agreed and began to strip while straddling Billy.

About eight minutes later Britt rolls off of Billy and both are laying side by side. Billy apologized for not going longer but he couldn't help himself once he felt it. Britt assured him that it was fine and that they would just have to try again. Billy nodded and looked at the clock. "Ohh shit, I need you to take me home if you want to be back in time to beat your parents. They had ended up laying there for over an hour even though the conversation only took about five minutes.

Billy was dropped off and Britt raced back to her house. Once inside Billy went straight to Johnny's room where he bragged about his time with Britt and how her parents almost caught them which made it even crazier. Johnny congratulated Billy and both talked about how each one was a Rockstar at sex.

Britt told Maddy everything and the two girls talked about how weird and short it was and wondered if that is how all boys were at first or if it was just those two. Comparing them to some of the videos they had seen on the internet.

Time went on and all of them found that things change over time and that the first-time awkwardness would soon turn into bright smiles and breathless wishes.

CHAPTER 11

START OF ADULTHOOD

With a few weeks left of the school year Trish and Dean asked the boys to sit down for a discussion that they would probably not like to have. Dean and Trish informed the boys that they would not be able to go through summer and not have jobs. The boys looked devastated and Johnny asks "WHY?" Dean tells them that they need to start paying their dues because after high school they would need to start paying their own way.

Both their faces went blank as they tried to find any excuse for why they shouldn't have to, but neither one had anything good enough, they just sighed and slumped down in the chairs. Dean and Trish get up and leave the two to their thoughts. The two boys begin discussing what type of job they wanted, how much they were hoping to get paid, days they would work, etc.

The next day the boy's told their girlfriends what was going to happen and that they had no choice in the matter. Britt was happy because she thought about getting a job also, Maddy was less than happy because now she wouldn't get to see Johnny that much. Maddy did ask when they were going to start looking for a job, Johnny told her that they were going to start that afternoon to see what's available.

A few weeks went by with no luck on finding a job when Johnny came across a movie theatre ad that was looking for a few people for the summer. Johnny told Billy and they both filled out an application online, later that day Billy found a small amusement park that needed help running the rides and games, they both decided to apply for that one as well.

The first one to call them for an interview was the amusement park and scheduled it on the following Thursday after school. Then the next day the theater called and scheduled an interview for that Friday, just when they thought all was good the boys received another call wanting to interview the two boys as paralegal trainees. Apparently, Dean thought the boys could use some help with the job search and put them in for a training program for the firm he worked for. The boys were happy to have three interviews in the same week and couldn't wait to see if they would get the job or jobs.

The day came for their first interview and the boys went in their Sunday best. The first job offered $7.25 hr. starting pay, working four days a week, afternoon to evening times, with variable off days. The boys seemed less than thrilled about the pay and the days but were happy to find out they could ride and play games for free. They were told that the company would call them in a day or two to tell them if they would be offered the job. The next day the boys went to the first interview at the law firm and were told that the pay was $8.50 hr. Monday thru Friday 9 to 5. The boys liked that the pay was better but working 5 days a week was less than appealing to them, plus no additional perks. The boys rushed to their next interview, which was the theater, there they were told that pay was $7.35 hr. working three to four days a week mostly afternoon and nights.

After it was all said and done the boys didn't know what to do. The pay wasn't the best however the perks were not that bad at the theater and amusement park. The pay was better, but the number of days and lack of perks were not. Plus, they thought what if one calls and they turn it down but then no one else calls, then they would be right back at square one.

The boys talked about it and they both wanted to work together so they would have each other as back up, but at same time they were undecided on which job they wanted. This was becoming more stressful than searching for a job.

The following day all three places called offering them the job, both decided to turn down the paralegal job but that was the only one they agreed on. Johnny took the job at the theater and Billy the one at the amusement park. This ended up working to both of their advantage, one would get them into movies free and the other one would give them free rides and games.

School ended and the boys were now a few days into their summer jobs, and everything appeared to be working out. They both worked the same days mostly and very similar hours. Their girlfriends would come by and visit occasionally, and they would spend all their off days with each other. They saved up a little money out of every paycheck throughout the summer until they were able to pull enough money together and buy a used car to share.

Dean took the boys to the used car dealer and helped the boys navigate the car buying process. They looked around and test drove a few cars before settling on a late 90's Civic. Some minor body work but all in all it was in good condition.

Both the boys excelled at their jobs and sharing the car became a chore but neither one minded. Johnny and Billy were given raises near summer's end and offered a permanent position for the fall and winter seasons due to their work ethic. Both accepted graciously and were happy that they would have money during their senior year of high school.

CHAPTER 12

THE LIFE CHANGING DECISION

Summer ended and the school year began. The boys were busy with school, their girls and their jobs which made their senior year seem like it moved by faster than previous ones did. Before they knew it, winter break was approaching, and school would soon be out for the holidays.

Near the end of the week before winter break the boys were headed to the cafeteria when they noticed a table set up with military stuff on it, and behind the table stood a guy in uniform. Curiosity got the best of the boys, they approached the soldier and started asking who he was and what he was doing. The soldier behind the table introduced himself as Sgt. Walters with the U.S. Army and that he was there to recruit people.

The boys scoffed at the idea for a second, thinking this guy can't be serious. Then the Sgt. Walters asked the boys the one question that would make them reflect on everything. "So, what are your plans for after high school?" The boys looked at each other and back at the Sergeant and just shrugged. The Sergeant then offered the boys a pamphlet to go over and bid them a good day as they walked into the lunchroom.

Britt and Maddy joined the two of them at their table and could see the gears turning in their heads. "What has you two bothered?" Maddy asked. Johnny looks up from the pamphlet in his lap and says "Well, we don't know what we are gonna do after high school." Britt chimed in and told them that she was planning on attending UGA, in Athens, Ga. Maddy said that she was going to take a year off and enjoy life for a while before she settled on anything. Britt then asked Billy what he was going to do, but Billy still looking at the pamphlet shrugged and mumbled "I don't know." The rest of the day Billy and Johnny were lost in thought about what they wanted to do when they graduated. They never gave it much thought; they couldn't keep working where they were and college didn't seem like it was for them.

After the holidays Johnny started talking more about what he wanted to do with Billy and trying to plan the best course of action. College would have been too expensive, finding a better paying job would take time and no guarantees. Joining the military would guarantee him a job and other benefits, but it would take him away from home, not to mention he would probably get sent overseas.

Billy voiced some of the same concerns but talked Johnny into just relaxing about it for now, because they still had a few months left to figure it out. Johnny put his thoughts into the back of his mind to try and focus on the here and now.

As with the first part of the year, the second part seemed to fly by as well, before they both knew it, they were down to their final two months. Johnny began to stress more about what to do and Billy was beginning to become more worrisome himself. Johnny decided to talk things over with Maddy to see what she thought, she had no idea what he should do and told him she would support him either way.

Billy did talk to Britt, but she told him it was his decision and that she would not talk him into something he didn't truly want to do. Billy thanked her and continued to contemplate what he wanted to do in his life.

Both of the boys wanted to do something more than what they were doing now with their life and do something that would allow them to bring out their full potential. They just weren't sure what it would or could be.

When Johnny got home after school one day, he found himself rummaging through some drawers of his desk looking for his resume that he made in school as a project, when he came across the pamphlet, he was given by the Army Sergeant. He looked it over again and seriously thought about what it would be like if he joined.

Billy arrived home a short while later after visiting Britt at her after school job and found Johnny writing in a notebook. Curiosity got the best of him, and he decided to ask "Hey, What cha writing?" Johnny looked up and told him "I am writing Pros and Cons of joining the Army." Billy became more intrigued and asked if he could see what he had so far. Johnny obliged and showed Billy his list and told him that he was seriously considering it. Billy asked where he found all his information for his list and Johnny told him he had gotten on his computer and looked it up.

Johnny made a good case for Billy to consider joining also. Johnny told Billy that he was going to take a week or two to think about it and make his decision. By then they would only have a month left and would have time to change his mind if he decided to go for it.

Billy said he would think about it also and asked Johnny to tell him first so that way they could sign up together if he decided to.

Later on, Billy was talking to Britt on the phone after she got off work and was telling her all the things that he discussed with Johnny and told her that he was pretty sure that he would join even if Johnny didn't. Britt expressed her concerns about it but also told him that she would always be by his side no matter what he chose. Billy was happy to hear her say that and they continued to talk for a little while longer before heading off to bed.

About a week and a half later Johnny met up with Billy before he headed off to work for his Saturday shift and told him that he was going to join the Army. Billy smiled and said that he decided that he was going to join the day after they talked about it but didn't say anything to Johnny so that way, he wouldn't influence his decision. Johnny smiled and said great they could join together and support each other if they needed it. They both talked about and decided that they would tell Johnny's parents at dinner later and then Billy's dad the next day.

Sitting at the dinner table that evening Johnny told his parents that he and Billy needed to tell them something. Dean and Trish put their forks down and gave Johnny their attention. Johnny proceeded to tell them that he has decided to join the Army and Billy would be joining also. Trish was less than pleased with this announcement and was visibly upset. Dean on the other hand was more content then anything. An awkward silence fell over the table as Trish went back to eating and Dean thought about what he had heard. Johnny was becoming nervous and felt the weight of his decision and how it had affected his family.

Dean finally broke the tension by telling Johnny that he was proud of the decision he made and that he will assist him in any way he needs. This made Johnny smile, but his mom now stared at Dean, giving him the evil eye.

After dinner Trish called for Dean to come with her so she could "TALK" with him. Dean followed as she led him to the kitchen. Johnny and Billy could overhear the both of them as Trish was really giving it to Dean about his support for Johnny's decision and wonder why he wasn't as scared for him as she was. Upon hearing this Johnny decided to go in the kitchen and try to comfort her and let her know that he would be fine.

After talking for a few minutes Trish finally gave into the fact that Johnny was no longer a little boy and that he was capable of making this decision on his own and that she would support it as well.

Billy went to bed that night hoping that telling his dad wouldn't be as dramatic as telling the Lang's

The next day Billy and Johnny got ready to surprise Sam and tell him of Billy's decision. They pulled up to Sam's apartment and made their way to the door. Billy was growing excited as he knocked on his dad's door.

Sam opened the door shocked to see Billy there at 11 in the morning. "Billy?... What are you doing here today?" He said confused. Billy with excitement says, "I got something I want to tell you." Sam turns quickly looking inside then back at Billy and ask's "I thought you weren't planning on visiting till next week?" Billy quickly responds, "I wasn't, but then I made this decision and I wanted to share it with you."

Sam met a woman a few months ago and was seeing her on a regular basis. He informed her of his past and about his current situation and asked if she was ok with dating someone with his baggage. She didn't mind and offered him a deal that she wouldn't push to meet his son as long as he stayed the man she met.

Sam, growing anxious asks, what it was, that Billy needed to say hoping that he wasn't being too suspicious, keeping the boys from entering. Billy's excitement kept him distracted as he finally tells his father "I'm joining the Army with Johnny." Sam looks at both of them, then says, "That's great Billy, I am proud of you. We should get together when you have more time and talk about it." Billy began to grow suspicious now and then from out of nowhere he hears "Hey sweetie, who's at the door?" Billy's eyes pop and his mouth drops as fear and anger fill him "WHO is that?" he asks. Sam quickly tries to explain as Billy pushes the door open looking in and seeing a woman slightly younger than his dad standing at the entrance of his dad's bedroom dressed in a robe. All of Billy's anger found its way to the front of Billy's mind and it all came out in one harsh protest. "What the FUCK. First mom dies, so you send me away with grandma and grandpa. Secondly, I come back home, and you decide to beat me because you can't live with yourself. Third, you say you have gotten better but when it came to me living with you, you didn't want me. Finally, after all this time of trying to keep in touch with you and let you be a father figure, you decide to replace mom with... with this bimbo and don't even tell me." Sam tried interjecting while Billy was going off but to no avail, so when Billy finished Sam try to explain to Billy who and what and why he kept her a secret. However, Billy wasn't listening as he spoke the last bit of his mind "I hate you and don't want to see you ever again." Sam tried to stop Billy as he turned away and raced back to the car. Johnny followed behind and tried to comfort Billy and calm him down. The only thing he could get Billy to say was "I can't wait to leave this shit town."

CHAPTER 13.

START OF A NEW CHAPTER IN LIFE

Johnny told Maddy a few days later and Britt confirmed with Billy that he was still going through with it. Both girls supported their boyfriends and were happy for them for figuring out what they were going to do after high school.

With two weeks left of school Johnny and Billy drove to the Army recruiting office after class one day. They entered the office and became extremely nervous about what they were about to do. "Hello men" a voice came from behind a computer. "Hey." "Hello." They replied, a soldier in uniform popped up from behind the computer and waved the boys over to his desk. The boys recognized the man from the school cafeteria as Sgt. Walters.

The boys sat down as Sgt. Walters asked the boys how he could help them. Unsure of how all this worked the boys told him they were interested in joining the Army and wanted to know what type of job they could get. Sgt. Walters told them that they first had to take a test known as the A.S.V.A.B. and depending on the score they received, determined what they could qualify for. The boy's looked at each other and asked where they were supposed to go and take the test. Sgt. Walters just laughed and told them that they take the test there in the office, they had computers set up so they could take the test and get their score instantly.

Sgt. Walters led the boys over to the computers and gave them all the information they needed to enter and how the test worked. He then left to go back to his desk and wait until the two boys finished their tests.

Johnny finished the test first and went back to the desk and sat down with Sgt. Walters, a short time later Billy finished and joined them. Sgt. Walters retrieved the results and pulled up a list of jobs that they qualified for. Their test scores were just above average and qualified them for a multitude of jobs that the Army offered. Billy did score a little lower than Johnny, so he had slightly fewer jobs available. They still had a lot they could choose from that they both qualified for. They talked it over and pointed to one of the jobs on the list and Sgt. Walters verified that they did in fact qualify for it and searched on his computers for opening slots. After a few seconds he told them that he could get one in there now and then maybe next month could get the other one in.

Sgt. Walters was trying to fill in the mass open slots that the infantry had due to the high rate of departures. When the boys pointed to a job that was not suffering from lack of people he would manipulate Johnny and Billy by telling them anything that would turn them away.

The boys shook their head and pointed to another job on the list 19K and asked what job that was. Sgt. Walters smiled and asked the boys "You know what tanks are right?" The boys shook their heads with excitement. Sgt. Walters continues "Well you will mostly be washing them and keeping them clean for inspections." The boy's smiles quickly disappeared. They looked over the list again and found another job that was on both their lists, they ask "What is an 89D?" Sgt. Walters had a more serious look this time and told them "Well boys, that job requires you to wear large heavy suits and try to make bombs the enemy have explode." Johnny and Billy quickly shook their heads no. They decided to ask what job they could get and be together but also a job that would be more interesting than the other ones they had picked out.

Sgt. Walters smiled and played on his computer for a second and finally came back with an answer "Well, the only job I can guarantee that I can get both of you in at the same time is 11B." The boys looked at their list and saw it on both and asked what the job was. Sgt. Walters being as cunning as he can says "Well you would be keeping up foreign relations with host nations and ensuring a stable friendly cultural exchange of ideas." The boys looked at each other and talked about how cool that sounded, they then took some time and finally agreed to sign up for 11B and become soldiers.

The boys signed all of their initial paperwork and were then given a schedule of events for them, they would need to do before they could ship off to basic training. The first of which was being medically evaluated. Then they would have to take a provisional PT test. Then report to the recruiting office for drill instruction before finally being sent off. It would be a few weeks since they still had some school left and the Army had to make sure that they had their diploma's before leaving.

The next few weeks went by and the boys were getting more excited and scared as they came closer to leaving. They passed their PT test and were cleared medically. The drill practice was easy as all they did was learn how to face direction and walk in step with each other.

Johnny's parents were also becoming more anxious because soon their first born was going to be leaving the nest along with their unofficial adopted son. Dean tried to be stoic but Trish was a wreck and did everything she could to baby her sons while they were still home.

Johnny and Billy received their ship out date for June 17, from the Military Entrance Processing Station or MEPS station in Atlanta. The recruiter would drive them up a day early and stay at a hotel that the Army specified, then be picked up in the morning and be shuttle to the MEPS station before swearing in and leaving for basic training. Parents and other family members were welcomed to come to the MEPS station and watch the swearing in ceremony and say goodbye to their new soldiers before seeing them again at graduation from Basic.

The 16th of June finally came and Johnny's parents followed the boys to the hotel and waited for them to check in before taking them out to eat and celebrate their next steps forward in life.

The boys went to bed that night restless and couldn't contain their excitement or their nerves. They did get to sleep late that night only to be woken a few hours later by the wakeup call the Army had set for everyone in the hotel. The boys showered, got dressed and joined the other recruits' downstairs for breakfast before getting on the shuttle bus and going to the MEPS station.

When the boy's arrived, they were sent to stand in line and wait for their names to be called to sign their final paperwork and get their packets then wait for the swearing in ceremony.

Dean, Trish and Lilly all arrived at the time they were told to be there and met Billy while he waited for his name to be called. They talked for a few minutes and discussed the small things in life while Billy waited. Johnny came out of the office area with his paperwork packet and joined his parents and Billy. They were talking for a few minutes when Billy was called back, returning a few moments later.

Trish was becoming more emotional as time got closer and just about lost it when another person in uniform called all the recruits in to form up for the ceremony. A small stage stood against the back wall and centered, the room's occupants stood in formation facing the stage. A Colonel approached the stage as a Sergeant called everyone to attention. All the recruits snapped their heels together and placed their arms straight down their sides with their hands in a fist. The parents lined the back of the wall and watched as all the recruits raised their right hands and recited the oath of service.

After the ceremony the recruits had five minutes to say their goodbyes before getting on the bus that would take them away to Basic Training. Trish cried and Dean did his best to hold it together even though in his mind he was crying as well. The boys finished their goodbyes, shook hands with Dean, hugged Trish and kissed Lilly on the cheeks before making their way their way to the bus.

In a parked car in the lot across the street from the bus, two girls stood waving their hands in the air as they watched their boyfriends get on the bus. Johnny was taking his seat when he noticed the two girls and quickly got Billy's attention. Johnny then slid the window open and began waving back at Maddy and Britt.

Maddy and Britt got the information from Johnny's parents were going to surprise the boys by coming to say goodbye. Maddy overslept a little and was rushing to pick up Britt and then hit traffic which delayed them from getting there earlier. The girls were worried that they would miss them before they left, Maddy had pushed her car almost to the limits on the interstate praying not to get a ticket. When they pulled into the MEPS station they saw a group of people walking out of the building and feared it was already too late. They were about to leave when Britt spotted Johnny walk out the door. They began jumping up and down trying to get their attention as he and Billy walked to the bus.

The bus pulled away as the boys still had their faces placed out the window and watched as everyone moved out of sight before turning back in their seats for the ride to Fort Benning.

Trish and Dean spotted Maddy and Britt and walked over to their car to greet the girls. Trish was still wiping tears from her eyes as they talked about the ceremony and how emotional it was to watch the boys leave. This caused Maddy and Britt to become teary eyed as well and commented about how much they were going to miss them.

A couple of hours later the bus approached Fort Benning and pulled up to a building where three uniformed personnel were waiting. The bus stopped and one of the Soldiers got on the bus and immediately began shouting instructions. When the Drill Sergeant was finished everyone was hurrying to get off the bus, get their bags and make their way inside.

They were introduced to the Drill Sergeants that would guide them through the reception process and ensure that they had everything done and ready for the start of their Basic Training unit. During this week they would receive their shots, fill out more paperwork, and get clothing issued. This week would be the easiest week for the next 12 weeks. After this, things would become more tense and stressful for everyone.

The routine for the week was easy. First, they would wake up and go to breakfast, then march everyone to whichever appointment was scheduled for the day, then they would take everyone to lunch followed by the afternoon appointments, then dinner before having down time to shower and clean up before bed. Everyone was gaining a false sense of security with the belief that this was how the whole time was going to end up being throughout Basic. They were mistaken and would soon find out just how mistaken they were.

The night before the last day the Drill Sergeants that were in charge of the group told them that they would be going to their training unit after breakfast and that the uniform would be the Army Combat Uniform or ACU's for short, they would need to make sure everything was packed and ready to go.

The next morning everyone woke up to the standard yelling of the Drill Sergeants and got dressed. Next, they had everyone take their belongings and issued items to the receiving yard, which was a large concrete pad, located next to the barracks before taking them all to breakfast. After breakfast they marched everyone to the receiving yard where they retrieved their personal belongings bag and then sat them down and told them to wait.

Small talk broke out amongst the group and Johnny and Billy started wondering what would happen once they arrived at their training units. The other boys they met all chimed in on their thoughts when a line of buses pulled up beside the group.

The three buses caused a hush to come over everyone and when the doors opened, a Drill Sergeant came off of each bus and made their way to the front of the formation. One went and talked to the head reception Drill Sergeant and the other two began picking random people out of the group and taking them over to the baggage area.

It seemed like an hour had passed and the selected people had loaded bags and drove off on trucks with other Drill Sergeants that brought the trucks over. The main three stood off to the side and watched as if they were waiting for something. Small talk once again broke out, as the group of recruits were becoming nervous with anticipation.

Suddenly the head Drill Sergeant walked to the front of the group and with a voice that sounded stressed and intimidating began shouting *"Everyone listen up and shut your mouths. My name is Drill Sgt. Hunt. I will be your Head Drill Sergeant for the next twelve weeks of your lives. Over to your left is Drill Sgt Gaul and Drill Sgt Henderson. They will be one of your platoon Drill Sergeants."* A couple of people didn't quite get the memo about shutting up as some voices could be heard coming from the crowd. Drill Sgt. Hunt did not like this one bit as his attitude changed drastically as he turned towards the direction of the noise and began shouting even louder *"Oh, I'm sorry. I didn't mean to interrupt your important meeting. Please allow me to give you some of my time to replace the time I took from you."* The group that had been conversing quickly got silent and did their best to avoid eye contact. Drill Sgt. Hunt watched the group for a few minutes before turning back to the rest of the formation and continuing. *"Alright, now that their meeting is over, we can continue. When I point to your row, I will assign that row a number. That number will correspond with the bus in line. One will be the first bus and so on. Once I assign all the numbers, I will call out each row individually and you will stand up, place your personal bag facing forward, you will then do a left face and proceed to the bus you're assigned and fill it from the back to the front. Once on the bus you will sit with your hands placed on your knees and be quiet."* The Drill sergeant went through and assigned all the rows numbers. The first 3 rows were number one and next three were number two and the last 4 rows were number three. Johnny and Billy were in a row assigned to the second bus.

When their number was called the row stood up, placed their bags facing forward, faced left and then moved to the bus they were assigned to. Johnny and Billy ended up near the middle of the bus and watched as the rest of the people got on and sat down. Johnny wanted to say something, but fear kept him quiet as he didn't want to upset the Drill Sergeant at the front of the bus.

It took a few minutes of quiet observation before some people started questioning what was going on. One person could be heard saying "The busses must be full, what are we waiting for?" and as if by some superhuman hearing ability, as soon as he said it a Drill Sergeants hat appeared on the steps as he made his way up the steps. Everyone quickly became quiet and faced forward as the Drill sergeant stared at everyone. Not saying a word, he turned to the driver and gave her the sign that he was ready.

The first bus began to pull away followed by the other busses. Everyone sat quiet and feared what might happen next.

A few minutes into the ride the Drill Sergeant turned back to everyone and said *"Listen up, I'm Drill Sgt. Henderson. When we stop you will have 10 seconds to vacate the bus and file in under the second overhang."* He then turned back to the front and waited. A few minutes went by and the bus finally approached a large brick building. The building had a center point that looked like a lobby with a desk in the entrance. Two wings were coming off from the center point that had open bays underneath.

The bus stopped and the door opened. The Drill Sergeant turned and began yelling *"Get OFF my bus, 10. 9. 8. You're not moving fast enough. 7. One legged hobbits move quicker. 6. 5. I don't think, you think, I am serious. 2. Faster. 1."* While the Drill Sergeant was yelling, everyone was struggling to move fast enough to get off the bus.

Billy and Johnny stumbled to the second bay and formed up with the rest of the people. They could hear all of the other Drill sergeants yelling at people that were still making their way off the other busses and to their respective areas.

Once everyone was where they were supposed to be, the Drill Sergeants directed everyone to place their bags on the ground to the left of their person. Then the Drill sergeants yelled that they failed to meet the time limit and they were all going to pay, as he ordered them into the push-up position and to begin doing push-ups. He bellowed out the cadence "Down, up, down, up, down, up." He continued on for a short time, ensuring everyone knew that they were no longer going to be coddled.

CHAPTER 14

BASIC TRAINING

After doing twenty-five push up the Drill Sergeants ordered them back to their feet and to the position of attention. Drill Sgt. Hunt walked to the center of a pit that was covered with little black chunks of rubber and stepped up on a pedestal in the center. He then pointed to the opposite corner of the pit from where the recruits stood, where a pile of green duffle bags that all of their issued items had been stacked in a pyramid pile.

He gave them to the count of fifteen to get their bag and get back in formation. He started counting with no warning and the whole company of recruits began to frantically run to the pile and pull bags off looking for their names and threw the ones off to the side that were not theirs. When the Drill Sergeant was down to five everyone raced back to their individual platoons with only a handful carrying bags.

Drill Sgt. Hunt informed everyone that they had failed again and proceeded to make them do more pushups. After twenty or so push-ups, he gave them a count of ten to get their bags and get back in line. Again, he started counting but this time at a faster pace as everyone raced to find their bags again. When he reached 5 again everyone raced back with less people carrying bags then the first time. Drill Sgt. Hunt made everyone do more push-ups, after about fifteen he had them stand up and told them that he guessed

"I thought I was getting people who wanted to be soldiers but instead it just looked like I got a bunch of weekend campers. I have seen girl scouts more organized than yall are." He then told them that he would give them a break and allow them the count of twenty-five to get their bags, since they didn't want to do what they were told the first time. He started counting again and everyone rushed back over. This time a few people started calling the names on bags they picked up and tossed them to the people that answered. Upon hearing the group start working as a team, Drill Sgt. Hunt slowed his count down a little to give them a few extra seconds. This lasted two more times before everyone had their bag and was in formation.

After that was all said and done Drill Sgt. Hunt introduced everyone to the company's First Sergeant, 1SG. Sanchez. 1SG Sanchez stepped up on the podium and told everyone what he expected and what they should expect from him and his Drill Sergeants. At the end of his brief he introduced the company's commander Captain, Grosslin. The commander gave a very short speech and then turned things back over to the 1SG who in turn, turned it back over to the Drill Sergeants.

Each platoons Drill Sergeant directed their platoons to the bay that they would be staying in for the next twelve weeks. The first group which was also first platoon was the one to Billy and Johnny's right, was on the floor just above their heads. Johnny and Billy's platoon was second platoon, they were directed to go up to the second floor above them to find a bunk and place their bags on the mattress. Johnny's platoon rushed up the stairs and everyone rifled through the bay finding a bunk, Johnny and Billy were lucky enough to find one they could share and placed their bags down quickly before someone else could.

Drill Sgt. Henderson came up shortly after and called everyone to a semi-circle or school circle, around him as he pulled up a chair and sat down. Everyone else sat crossed legged on the floor as he instructed, then proceeded to teach them all the standard for their wall lockers, laundry bags, bed set ups and formation position. He then had them fill out cards with personal information, along with next of kin and emergency contacts. After that was done, he had them write a letter and put certain information about the company and platoon they were assigned to and also the base address and the format of how to write so their parents and loved ones would be able to write letters to them. They then placed the letter in an envelope and put their home address on it.

Once they finished the letter, they were instructed to go back to their bunk and retrieve their personal bag and place them at the corner of the beds. They then proceeded to inventory the bags and all hygiene items were removed and placed on their beds and all other items were placed back in the bag. Each person filled out an inventory sheet and placed one copy in the bag and one copy went to the Drill Sergeant and they kept the last copy. They then went through their issued items and placed them where the Drill Sergeant instructed them to.

The rest of the day involved lunch and then more issued items for field training, bed linen and instructional time. Johnny and Billy both believed that this was going to be a cake walk, if all they had to do was a few push-ups and sit around and listen to the Drill Sergeants speak all day.

Dinner came and the company marched over to the dining facility aka DFAC and got in line to get food. The layout was far more appetizing then the lunch was, desserts were now available and the meal selection appeared more appetizing. Johnny saw a slice of apple pie and thought about how delicious it looked and planned on grabbing it when he got down to that area. As he made his way down the line, he would look up to see if it was still there hoping to get that he would be able to get it.

He was only a few people away when he saw another soldier pick it up and place it on their plate, Johnny was saddened slightly because it was the last apple pie slice and he didn't really want the other ones that were up there. Billy, who was behind him, nudged him and mimed don't worry about it as they left the line to find a seat.

The Drill Sergeants took turns eating, half would eat while the others walked around watching everyone, then they would swap out so that the others could eat. One of the Drill Sergeants was walking by Johnny looking over everyone's shoulder when suddenly *"Oh, would you look at this. Someone must be celebrating a special occasion."* The Drill Sergeant said, other Drill Sergeants made their way to the table and all started to join in, *"Holy shit Private. Is that an apple pie. You must be living the good life."* One Drill Sergeant said, then quickly followed by another saying *"Man you must be rich. I wish I could afford such delicacy on a Drill Sergeants pay. I envy you Private."* A third Drill Sergeant started to speak when the soldier pushed the pie off his tray which stopped the Drill sergeant in mid-sentence to then say *"Oh. You don't want it now. Are you afraid it will affect your figure. Well Private don't worry, we can help you maintain your girlish figure. Go ahead and eat the pie Private."* The Private just placed his head down in shame hoping that this would end when the company First Sergeant walked up and in a stern voice said *"Private, we don't waste food in my Army. You picked up that pie, now you are gonna eat that pie."* The Private hesitantly took the pie and proceeded to eat it while the Drill Sergeants went back to berating him *"MMM… That sure looks tasty. Is it tasty Private?"* At this point he was almost in tears when it was time for the Drill Sergeants to swap.

When the first group of Drill Sergeants got up from eating, the ones surrounding this poor Private all left and went to the line to get their food. Everyone thought it was over until Drill Sgt. Hunt, who was one of the first Drill Sergeants to eat, began yelling for everyone to get up clean their trays and form up outside. The other Drill Sergeants who were done eating began yelling at everyone to move faster as they got up and bumping into each other made their way to the tray drop off area and then outside.

Once everyone was formed up Drill Sgt. Hunt addressed the company saying *"Alright everyone, in consideration of Private Pie's celebratory day, and his concern for his figure. We will take the scenic route back to the barracks."* Drill Sgt. Hunt then proceeds to call the company to a double time march and take them on a 2-mile-long jog. About halfway through the route, one person fell out of formation and began puking. After short distance later another person followed suit. When they were close to the end of the run Private Pie fell out and began puking like the others. The rest of the group finished the run, but they were all experiencing some sort of stomach pains. As one of the other Drill Sergeant's was gathering the stragglers and bringing them to meet up with everyone else.

The routines for the next three weeks were pretty tame in overall terms and followed a standard routine. Wake up at five in the morning, do physical training (PT), go to chow, then team building exercises, basic self-defense training, chow again, the standard classes the Army designates as mandatory such as sexual harassment, etc., then dinner chow with remedial PT for people that needed extra help and instructional time for everyone else then down time before bed at nine. Basic was divided up into three phases, Red, White and Blue.

One of the highlights during that first few weeks was the gas chamber. Johnny and Billy ended up being one of the first in line to go through the gas chamber. The first group placed their gas masks on their faces when instructed then entered the building in a single file line circling the outer wall until there was no space available along the wall. Staring through the lens of the mask they could see the room was lit by a dim light hanging in the center. The Drill Sergeants inside the room began giving the instructions for what they would have to do before leaving the chamber. Johnny doesn't remember much about what exactly happened after he removed his mask and had taken a deep breath in. All he knew was once the air hit his lungs, fire filled his chest as tears blurred his vision and mucus began to pour from his nose. Billy didn't do any better as he felt like his lungs were melting and his flesh was covered in tiny shards of glass.

After they all met the required instruction they were led out of the chamber without their mask on. They could hear others laugh at the site of group as they exited flapping their arms and trying to fill their lungs with fresh clean air. A few minutes went by before their vision began to clear and they were able to enjoy the site as the others went through and suffered the same fate they did.

Another highlight for the boys was Victory Tower, a tall structure that had a rappelling wall, a rope bridge going up, a single rope that soldiers had to balance laying on top of going down and a staggered level terrace that they had to navigate to get to the top in order to rappel. Billy and Johnny enjoyed the rope bridge and rappelling the most, as well as watching other trying to do it and freaking out because of the height or losing their footing trying to move across the ropes and falling to the net below them.

The first few weeks ended with an overnight field exercise where they went over basic patrol formation and advanced them from red phase to white phase.

The second few weeks were focused on weapon proficiency and combat drills. Billy and Johnny loved shooting and found it easy to familiarize themselves with their weapons. They had played war games on their gaming console but neither one of them actually shot a real gun. This was a new opportunity that they truly enjoyed having and became fairly proficient at it.

On qualification day they decided to compete with each other and see who could get the closest to 40 out of 40 which would be perfect in qualification. Billy was first of the two to shoot and took his place on the firing line at lane 8.

The qualification range had pop up targets starting at 25 yards up to 300 yards. Each shooter would have just a few seconds to aim at their target and fire before it would fall on its own and count as a miss. There were a total of 15 firing lanes for shooters to use, to the rear of the range were two sets of bleachers. One set was for shooters yet to qualify and the other was for shooters that had already qualified. To qualify the shooter had to hit 23 of the 40 targets, if not they would have to go again until they did.

After shooting from the three designated positions of prone supported, prone unsupported and kneeling, Billy's group stood up and waited for the results. The Drill Sergeant stationed in the control tower read out the numbers of the firing line positions and the scores, Billy grew anxious hearing the numbers as they called **"Lane 1, 28. Lane 2, 31. Lane 3, 22. Lane 4, 28. Lane 5, 33."** Billy's anxiousness grew as they were now two away from his number, **"Lane 6, 39. Lane 7, 26."** Finally, it was Billy's turn, **"Lane 8, 37."** Billy pumped his fist in the air and walked off the firing line smiling one of his biggest smiles. He teased Johnny as he walked past him and took his seat on the bleachers where the other shooters that qualified went. Johnny then made his way up to his position at lane 13 and prepared himself for engaging his targets. After he finished, he waited his number to be called, **"Lane 12, 19. Lane 13, 35."** Johnny was excited at first but then realized that he was two short of Billy's total. Billy didn't tease Johnny too much, because he knew that there were somethings that Johnny was going to be better at then he was.

Throughout the first few weeks of training both of the boys up to the point they were at now, found a new type of pride and accomplishment they haven't had before. Johnny knew Billy would be there for him in any situation and that would soon be proven

Two days after weapon qualification during mail call, Johnny's name was called three times instead of the normal two. Sometimes mail would back up and you might get two or three letters at the same time even though they were written on different days. Billy received his two letters, one from Dean and Trish and the other from Britt. Johnny was confused by receiving a third letter which happened to be from Maddy. Normally if he received a third letter it would be from his parents. When everyone found out he received two from the same girl they all knew that it was probably not good and teased him with the fact that it probably wasn't, Billy stepped in and tried to get everyone to leave him alone because they didn't know what it was about.

Billy put his letters on his bed and sat with Johnny as he opened Maddy's letters first. The first letter just talked about how much she missed him and how much she was enjoying her summer knowing she didn't have school later that year. She also mentioned how much she's been thinking about the future and how she can't wait to see what it has in store for her. Then Johnny got to the second letter and that's when his world turned upside down.

Billy could see all the color drain from Johnny's face and eyes flush with water. Johnny was clearly holding back tears and Billy could see it clear as day. The letter dropped from Johnny's hand and Billy quickly picked up. The rest of the platoon turned and went on about their business as if they didn't see anything. Billy glanced over the letter when a sentence caught his attention:

"I do love you Johnny, but I don't believe I am in love with you. I really believe we can be friends, but I don't think we can continue being boyfriend and girlfriend."

Billy tossed the letter aside and placed his hand on Johnny's back. Johnny's tears were forcing their way out and he was losing the battle on containing himself. Johnny stood up quickly and went into the latrine and closed himself in one of the stalls. Billy followed him into the latrine and sat outside his stall and tried to calm Johnny down. It took about an hour or so, but Billy finally calmed him down enough and he exited the stall. They both made their way to their bunk when Johnny turned to Billy and thanked him for his support and that he was going to show Maddy what she is missing out on. It still took him a little time to get over her completely and when he started to slack during training, Billy would pull him to the side and help him get his mind right and focused.

At the end of the second phase, they went on a three-day field exercise where they focused more on basic security, check points, and patrol tactics. By this time Johnny was completely rid of his thoughts of Maddy and was having fun again.

The last few weeks focused more on combat tactics and military drill and ceremony, followed by a PT test and a 5-day field exercise. Johnny got payback on Billy by scoring 90 percent on all the PT test events and awarded the Army PT patch. Billy had missed it by two pushups and 11 seconds on the run, Johnny teased Billy about as much as he was teased by him during weapon qualification.

The day before graduation Billy received an unexpected letter. When he opened it, he saw that it was from his father. He was tempted to just ball it up and throw it away immediately, but then decided to read it over. His father stated that he knew Billy was still upset with him, but he wanted him to know that he loved and was proud of his accomplishment. Billy then threw the letter away as if he never read it. He never told Johnny about it and kept it a secret from everyone. They both graduated from basic in the presence of Johnny's parents, little sister and Britt.

CHAPTER 15

A.I.T

After graduating Basic the boys didn't go far as they started their next level of training. The Army called it Advanced Individual Training, this consisted mostly of the same things they learned in Basic Training but on more in depth level as well as other tactics and procedures that were not covered in Basic. They were also trained in other weaponry system and radio communication, land reconnaissance, map reading and navigation, minefield safety and other things that they would regularly use at their main duty station. Most people when they graduated Basic would have to travel to another part of the base they were on or to an entirely different base. For Billy and Johnny, they didn't have to travel anywhere.

During this stage, they were still controlled by Drill Sergeants who were still tough when it came to training, but they seemed to have more free time where the Drill Sergeants didn't bother them and left them to themselves.

Another perk of being out of Basic was they were now allowed to go to the store during their free time on weekends without being watched consistently. The freedom they received was a sweet relief that Johnny and Billy had been missing especially when it came to the food, Johnny could now have his pie without repercussions.

About half of the people from their Basic Training unit were shipped off to other training areas for their respective job titles.

The other half were re-arranged into new groups for A.I.T except for Johnny and Billy who lucked out again and were placed in the same platoon again.

They both found training to be even better then Basic when it came to the field portion, but both struggled to stay awake during the PowerPoint classroom training, which was affectionally referred to as "Death by PowerPoint." All in all, they seemed to be blending into the Infantry as if it were meant for them.

Their favorite part was doing the land navigation course, running through the woods trying to find markers that were placed out there and beat the other teams that were doing the same.

A.I.T seemed to fly by quickly and before they knew it graduation was closing in quickly and their futures became uncertain. Not yet knowing where they would go or what they would be able to do once they arrived or what it would be like in the regular Army.

Johnny's family and Britt made the trip back to Ft. Benning and watched as their son, unofficial adopted son and boyfriend graduated from A.I.T. They were proud of both of them and scared at the same time because now they were no longer under the safety of training and subjected to the harsher reality of life in the Army.

Johnny and Billy received their orders at the end of the graduation ceremony and surprised to see that they were off to the 3rd Armored BDE, 1st BN, 8th INF RGT, Fort. Carson, Colorado. Trish was excited to hear that, since that meant the boys would at least be stateside for now.

Dean, Trish and Lily hugged the boys and said their goodbyes as they left to head back home, Britt hung around a little longer before having to leave. The boys went back to their barracks and finished packing for their trip out west the following day.

The morning came and Johnny was waiting outside the barracks while Billy was repacking one of his bags. Billy soon joined Johnny waiting for their bus to take them to the airport and start their chapter in life as Soldiers. The Drill Sergeants waiting with them no longer yelled or treated them as trainees or recruits but rather as fellow soldiers as they walked around and talked to all the graduates and answered questions that they had about being in the regular Army.

Johnny and Billy were called for their bus, along with a hand full of other soldiers and were soon on their way to the airport. Once they arrived, they made their way through security, to their gate. They boarded their plane and were off for their new unit.

Once the plane landed, they made their way through the terminal to the baggage claim area where they retrieved their bags. They looked lost as to what to do next they didn't quite know what to do now because no one actually told them what would happen once they arrived.

They stood around for a few minutes when another soldier approached them and called out "Hey, you guys headed to Ft. Carson?" Johnny turned to see a Sergeant walking up to them and nodded yes and then nudged Billy to turn and acknowledge the Sergeant.

The Sergeant greeted them and introduced himself "How are you guys doing? My name is Sgt. Gomez and welcome to Colorado. If you would please show me your orders, I will get you on the bus to your unit." Johnny and Billy pulled out a copy of their orders and showed them to Sgt. Gomez, who looked them over and then told them to follow him. He led the two to a row of busses and told them "You are on the third bus and it will be leaving in one hour. You can place your bags on the bus and go get something to eat inside the main terminal or wait on the bus."

Johnny looked at the time and saw that it was only 11am local but that would mean it was 1pm back at home. They decided to go ahead and grab a bite to eat before the bus headed off.

They finished eating and got to the bus with about twenty minutes to spare, there were a handful of other people on the bus all eager to see what the regular Army was like. They were all discussing what their Basic Training experiences and their A.I.T were like. They were getting to know each other while they waited for the bus to depart and all appeared to be happy about being out of training. The bus driver finally arrived and off they went to a new adventure ahead of them.

Due to the fact that the only experience they had in the Army was with Drill Sergeants and a lot of yelling and a lot of rushing around. As they got closer and closer to their destination everyone began to get more anxious.

After about two hours of driving, the bus pulled up to the gate of the base, everyone had their eyes glued to the windows as it pulled through and onto the base. A few minutes later the bus pulled up to a brick building, Johnny noticed that there were no Drill Sergeants, or any other Sergeants waiting for them and pointed it out to Billy.

The bus driver opened the door and stood up and announced, "Ok everyone, when you get off the bus you need to head into the building on the right." Billy looked around to see what everyone else was going to do, but everyone else looked confused too. Billy grabbed his bags and exited the bus followed by Johnny and then everyone else. They made their way to the building where they were greeted by the division staff duty personnel and directed where to wait until their unit representative came to collect them. Everyone was confused, including Johnny and Billy, "Man this is weird" Johnny said. Billy acknowledge and responded "Yeah, it kind of is. I mean no one is here yelling at us and everyone here seems so chill." Everyone talked and waited and slowly soldiers began to hear their names called and were taken off by other sergeants.

Another hour of waiting and finally a soldier called their names, "Pvt. Lang, Pvt. Derst." They both stood up and announced here. The soldier walked over and greeted the two, "Relax guys. I'm Staff Sgt. Peters and I am your platoon sergeant and I will be taking you guys to our unit and getting you set up." Relief and confusion overtook the two, here they had a Sergeant that was going to be in charge of them and he was laid back and spoke normal to them. They were not sure if they should smile or wait for the other shoe to drop and the yelling to start.

They arrived at their unit and SSgt. Peters took them to the company First Sergeant and company commander and introduced them, they got a standard welcome speech and a what to expect and what was expected of them speech as well. SSgt. Peters then took them to begin their in-processing and get their living quarters set up. That's when the two were split up, Johnny was going to be in First squad and Billy in third of the fourth platoon. Their rooms weren't far apart but it would be the first time in years that they would not be that close. Each room had a common room with four individual bedrooms. No one was around at the time due to being middle of the workday, so they had no idea of who their room mates were or what they were like.

They placed their bags down before being taken to their platoon, who was currently doing motor pool detail. SSgt. Peters called everyone over and introduced the two of them to the platoon before singling out their Squad leaders and informing them that from this point on they would be their first point of contact and they would also be the ones helping them complete the in-processing process.

CHAPTER 16

ALWAYS TRAINING

The two of them found themselves fitting in with their unit, by the end of the first month they had made some new friends and enjoyed the comradery that they had with the guys they were serving with. The veterans in the unit would haze them slightly but nothing to crazy. Being the new guys, they were given the shittier details which was to be expected. Weekends were a blast, because most of it was spent out partying and having fun and doing stupid things with their squad mates. Johnny was on the hunt trying to find a new girl or at least a temporary one, while Billy spent a lot of his down time talking to Britt on the phone when she was able to and trying to find a time for them to meet up.

Most of their days were spent doing details or training for combat. They still enjoyed it because now they were learning where exactly they fit in their squad, how their unit worked and also what their roles were going to be. They learned newer tactics and other ways of performing the basic ones that the older guys learned from firsthand experience.

The weather on the other hand they did not like. It was getting colder a lot earlier than it did in Georgia and that was one thing they did not enjoy at all. Their unit did a lot of mountain, house clearing and convoy training. They learned other roles within their squads and what happens if one goes down and how to cover down for that person.

As time went on the weather got colder, and snow began to fall. Britt flew out to Denver one weekend when she had a holiday break from college and Billy decided to take her on an overnight stay in Aspen and one day in downtown Denver before she had to fly back.

Johnny found himself out on the town with another soldier from his squad Private First Class or PFC. Adders, but everyone just called him by his first name Carl when out of uniform. The two of them were just waking up in the barracks from a night of partying in downtown Colorado Springs when Johnny decided to go get breakfast or lunch or whatever they were serving at whatever time it was from the DFAC, his hangover overpowered his ability to care about the time. He made his way through the line, when he happened to notice a female cook working in the back bringing out food trays to refill the salad selection. She appeared to be the same height and age as Johnny with red auburn hair and the looks that would have been an eight easily outside the Army. He made his way across the line and smiled at her when she looked up from restocking the cheese tubs. She gave a friendly smile back and then went on about her duties. Johnny sat down and was joined by other soldiers from his unit and they all talked about what their plans were for the day. Johnny couldn't take his mind off the cook as he stumbled through the conversation nauseated by his hangover.

Sunday afternoon Britt had left and Billy was back on base, Johnny was filling him in on the female that he had seen in the DFAC and how he was trying to figure out who she is so he could find out if she was seeing anyone.

A few days later rumors started floating around that they would be deploying by summer of the next year to Afghanistan. The platoon sergeant told everyone not to listen to rumors but to be expecting a deployment announcement sometime in the future because like every other unit they are scheduled for a rotation somewhere. Johnny informed his mom and dad and Billy told Britt even though they couldn't give them any details on when and where.

Another month went by and the announcement came that the unit would deploy around June of the following year to Afghanistan.

Billy and Johnny made it back home for a few days during Christmas and got to visit family and some of their friends from school. Johnny didn't bother to talk to Maddy or even look her up, Billy avoided his father as well. The trip in itself was still fun and getting away from everything was a great relief, as well as the warmer weather that Georgia had over Colorado.

When Johnny and Billy returned, they were informed that they would be going to the field for two weeks for training in three weeks. They were given a packing list and were told to make sure they had everything that was on the list and to pack anything extra in a carry bag or backpack.

The unit flew down to Fort Polk, Louisiana three weeks later. They went through convoy training and combat training as well as rifle marksmanship qualification and other similar training. They did a lot of the same things they were doing at their normal unit. This time they were also supported by 10th MNT Division Aviation regiment. Where they learned about helicopter insertion and extracts or known better by infill's and exfill's. Johnny and Billy enjoyed the training like every other time and really enjoyed the helicopter portion even though it scared them a little bit when the helicopter would suddenly drop down before climbing back to altitude and also how it shook when they were sitting on the ground.

Johnny was really happy to be in the field because it turned out that the dining personnel were on the same rotation as they were, and he got to see the female cook that had caught his eye.

One day during the training Johnny was considered to be a casualty and sent to kitchen detail for a day before rejoining his unit as a replacement soldier. During this time Johnny worked the courage up to talk with cook "Hi, I'm Johnny." She smiled and continued on her duties while Johnny began cleaning dishes. She returned a short time later with more dirty dishes for Johnny to clean, he tried to get more from her this time "So, I didn't catch your name earlier?" Johnny asked as she turned to walk away. She stopped for a second to see if he was still watching her walk away and decided to give him another smile before continuing on.

Johnny finished all the dishes and was beginning to sweep when she re-enters the back area to take a break. Johnny worked his way over to where she was sitting and asked her to move her feet so he could sweep. She looked at him then lifted her feet to allow him to sweep before saying "Did you really just go from the opposite side to here just to make me move my feet. Johnny just winked at her and kept sweeping while she watched.

She decided to give Johnny a little attention and said "Hi, I'm Claire." Johnny turned back and looked at her for a second before responding "Well, Miss Claire it's nice to meet you." Johnny said. Claire watched as Johnny started to make his way back over towards her just in time for her to stand up and say "Well breaks over. See you later ground pounder" as she walks out of the back and into the front.

Johnny couldn't get much more out of her the rest of that day, even though he tried every chance he got. When Johnny returned to his unit the next day, he told Billy all about it who encouraged him to keep trying because it seemed like she was playing hard to get but was into him.

The end of the training came, and the group boarded a plane back to Ft. Carson. Claire ended up sitting a few rows behind Johnny unbeknownst to him. When they arrived, Johnny felt someone push pass him on the plane and when he turned to see who it was, Claire just winked at him and kept moving forward trying to get off the plane. Johnny just smiled and turned to Billy and told him what happened and all he could say is "Dude, I told you she is playing hard to get." Johnny kept smiling grabbing his bag and following the crowd out of the plane.

On the bus ride back to base Johnny was checking his pockets for his phone, not remembering where he put it. When he reached his back pockets, he felt something awkward inside it. When he pulled it out, he realized it was a note. He opened it up and read *"Hey ground pounder. Call me some time. (719) 555-1172"* Johnny's eyes popped out of his head as shock took over him. He turned to Billy forgetting about looking for his phone and showed him the note. Billy smiled and announced to the other guys on the bus the Johnny was going to get laid that weekend. Everyone became rowdy and jokes started flying left and right and they all teased Johnny and one another.

Johnny called Claire the next day and asked her out on a date for the first weekend back. She accepted the invitation and told him that if he wanted to take her out, it had to be somewhere fun. He was trying to figure out what would be fun when it was 18 degrees outside and also what she thought was fun. "Hey, how am I supposed to know what is fun?" he asked in a text. She responds, "I guess you are going to have to talk to me and get to know me between now and our date." Johnny sighs and wondered why she just wouldn't tell him right then. "So, what do you like to do that's fun?" he text back. Claire smile and writes back "Ohh no GP. It's not going to be that easy." Johnny reads the message and asks "GP?" Her response was short "Ground Pounder." Johnny spent the rest of the week talking and texting her trying to get as much info he could.

He finally figured out that she liked ice skating, camping, fairs and hiking. Johnny decided that dinner, ice skating and maybe a slow walk under the stars might work. Saturday came and Johnny took her on the date. He had a good time but kept embarrassing himself by slipping on the ice while skating and walking. She had a great time with him and told him she would definitely be up for another date.

Johnny and Claire went on a few more dates and everything seemed to be going well, a matter of fact, it was going better than either one of them thought it would. Johnny enjoyed talking to

Claire and the level of sophistication she made him strive for, she enjoyed his boyish charms and middle school immaturity which made her laugh and how hard he dedicated himself to impress her. Claire was falling in love with Johnny and he was already head over heels for her.

The months seemed to roll by for Johnny and Billy and before they knew it, they only had two months left before deployment.

Johnny and Claire were out one weekend when Claire asked Johnny if he was scared about the deployment since he was an infantryman and would more than likely see combat. Johnny told her that he honestly hadn't thought about it because she was the only thing that was occupying his mind. She smiled and pulled him in closer to her and she went on to tell him her fears and that she never wanted to lose him. Johnny whispered in her ear that she never would and then in the shear passion of the moment said "MARRY ME."

Claire pushed back, shocked by what he said and asked, "Are you serious?" Johnny looked at her and said "Yeah. I love you and I want to marry you." Claire was more than happy to say yes but first she thought where they would do it and could they afford it but the next question she asked was "When do you want to do it?" Johnny already had an answer ready and said, "We can go to the courthouse and get married there before the deployment and when we get back, we can do the whole ceremony for family and friends." Claire thought about how long they had been dating and determined that she did love him in that way. "YES. Let's do it" She said proudly and for the rest of the night they planned out who they were going to tell and how to get the paperwork started.

A few weeks later Johnny and Billy were at the courthouse along with Claire and her friend Ebony waiting for their turn to go before the judge. The judge called them up and went through the marriage process and pronounced them husband and wife, once they were done, they signed their marriage certificate and Billy and Ebony signed the witness lines. The next workday, they submitted all the paperwork the Army required to update their records and adjust their pay accordingly.

The rest of the time went by quickly and they were soon ready for their deployment. Nerves were extremely high, and thoughts filled their minds on what to expect and what will happen once they were there.

CHAPTER 17

AFGHANISTAN

With only a few days to go before deployment, Johnny's and Billy's adopted family came out to see them for a few days and to see them off. Dean informed Billy that he told his dad about his deployment and hoped he held no ill will towards him for that. Billy shook his head and told him it was fine just let his father know not to expect anything from me. Dean shook his head and they both continued on with the family. Britt showed up the day after Johnny's parents and asked for a little alone time with Billy. Dean and Trish told them to take all the time they needed.

Johnny decided to introduce everyone to Claire but only as a girlfriend and not as his wife. Trish and Dean immediately approved of her and honestly thought that Johnny may have gotten lucky and got a girl that was out of his league. They didn't say that to him, but the thought did cross their minds. Johnny did meet Claire's family as well and both sides were able to sit down and eat together before their children left for Afghanistan.

The last few days were more of a blur as the only thing that any of them could remember was waving bye as they entered the bus and drove off to the airfield where they boarded a C17 Globemaster and departed across the world.

The first stop was in Kyrgyzstan where they waited for two days before boarding a C130 to Bagram Airfield. There, their unit went through country/culture familiarization training, as well as IED identification training and threat level assessments of the areas they were going to be operating in.

Afghanistan was mostly a mountainous region that had snowcapped peaks year-round. Most of the vegetation that covered the ground were shrubs, grass, agricultural farms with few trees that made up small forest areas. Mud and mortar houses and villages scattered the countryside, with few paved main roads. The main cities were built up a little more and had the majority of paved roads.

The bases they would be stationed out of, had larger concrete walls and hesco barriers, which were square wire mesh cages with an open top and fabric liner that you filled with dirt to create barriers or internal walls. The buildings were mixed between tent and wooden bunkers with few brick buildings. Everything was powered by large diesel generator that looked similar to truck shipping containers.

From Bagram they were sent to Jalabad or affectionately known as j-bad, where they would be based out of. Some of the unit would be sent out to other smaller forward operating bases (FOB's) throughout the region. The units would swap out with others to give relief to the personnel stationed out there and ensure that no one platoon or unit got screwed more than the others. Johnny and Billy's platoon were lucky enough to be held in J-bad for the time being.

Time didn't slow down or allow them to get to acclimated to their new surroundings before they were already scheduled for their first mission. A joint patrol with the outgoing unit to several small villages where the Army had a vested interest in maintaining good relations and protection from Taliban and other foreign fighting forces.

A few of the experienced guys helped Johnny and Billy learn the do's and don'ts of combat and tried to keep them calm when the time came for their convoy to roll out.

Four outgoing unit Humvees and 6 of Johnny's units set out on the patrol early in the morning to introduce the village elders to then unit commanders that would be taking over for the outgoing unit.

Johnny was in the second Humvee and Billy was seventh, as they rolled through the gates and out into country. Johnny was sitting back right of his vehicle staring consistently out the window. Billy ended up as gunner on this trip and was going back and forth from one side of the Humvee to the other praying he didn't have to use the mounted 50 cal. machine gun.

The patrol seemed to drag on as they made their way from one village to the next and then next. After the third village on the route, they were informed that another unit had made contact and was currently engaged with enemy fighters and was requesting assistance. The lead Humvee led the way trying to race to the unit under fire. It took about fifteen minutes to arrive at the location, where the unit under fire was set up in a defensive position. The enemy had broken contact a short time ago, but the fear of a second assault had them hold in their fortified position. Johnny's company commander exited his jeep and ordered everyone to dismount. Everyone except the gunners exited the vehicles and pulled security. The commander talked with the other units lead officer and offered to escort them back to their exfil position.

Everyone mounted back up and led the unit to their pickup location and then returned to base, due to the dying light and running low on fuel. Once back and debriefed, Johnny found Billy and talked about how crazy the day was with almost getting into combat. Carl who had one deployment already threw his arms over their shoulders and told them "that wasn't a crazy day and most days would probably end up like that." Carl walked off and Billy in a low voice whispered that he hopes that is the case.

Now that they were actually there, the whole, seems like a video game mentality finally left the boys. The fun, they had found at the start of their career was now gone. Replaced by realization that there was no guarantees or time outs to take a break or leaving when times get rough.

They went on two more patrols with no incidents before the outgoing unit finally left, leaving them to their own devices.

When not on patrol they spent their time at the gym, playing video games, writing to loved ones and watching movies. Johnny would sneak off to the DFAC where Claire was working and try to get her to sneak away for a little while. It worked only a few times but the fun of trying was enough to lighten their days.

Billy and Johnny were slowly no longer looked at like they were the new guys but looked at as one of the regular guys that had always been there. Soon they would earn their place among the others who already deployed without debate.

During the fourth week their platoon was being sent out to patrol a village further up the valley close to the border to gather intel on possible enemy movements in the region. They would be inserted via helicopter near one of the peaks and would have to travel down the mountain to the village.

Johnny loved the loud thud of the blades as they approached the large helicopter all the training they did prior to their deployment gave him a respect for the large beast. Entering from the ramp Johnny marveled at the room on the inside, Billy on the other hand hated the helicopters because they were too bumpy and loud.

Once they were all loaded, the roar of the blades as pitch was pulled filled the air and off, they went flying through the air. Johnny kept turning and looking out the window and envied the three gunners because this is what they got to do.

As they approached the Landing Zone (LZ) the crew chief gave them a 5-minute warning. They all checked their gear and prepped for landing. Then the crew chief gave them a 3-minute warning which they all then unbuckled from the seats. Then came the 30 second call and the ramp was raised from the level position and all eyes were focused on the back. A slight bounce from the wheels making contact and the ramp moving down was all they needed as they hurried to the rear and off the helicopter to the ground below. Once they exited, they all fanned out into a horseshoe around the back until everyone was unloaded and the helicopter lifted off.

The dust settled as the platoon leader called for a gear check and waited for the report. Once the report came in that everyone and all the gear made it off the helicopter, he ordered them to move out. Their platoon moved across the ridge following the easiest path they could down the mountain side.

A little over halfway the lead scout called back for the unit to hold position. The commander moved up and met with the lead scout and asked why he called for the hold. The scout informed the commander that he saw some movement in the tree line up ahead. The commander ordered his platoon to take up defensive positions and told first squad to check it out. Sgt. Kent, who led first squad, formed them up and moved them up to the wood line.

A random patrol by the Taliban was in the area when the echo from the helicopter was heard in the valley. They were searching for the area that they assumed it had landed and hoped to surprise the American force that may be in the area.

Billy watched as Johnny moved up ahead and said a little prayer for protection of his brother. As he disappeared into the woods a deafening silence fell over the remaining guys. You could hear a snowflake hit the ground as they waited and watched.

Inside the tree line Johnny was ever hesitant and his eyes darted around quickly at the slightest movement. They continued into the woods about a hundred yards and looked around for any sign of recent activity. After searching for about 10 minutes the squad leader was satisfied that there were no signs of anything and ordered the squad back to the platoon. As Sgt. Kent turned to head back, a loud crack rang through the air and hot metal tore through his right thigh. The rest of the squad turned back facing the direction of the shot as more and more shots peppered the air and splintered the trees. Johnny's training clicked in and he began returning firing, with the rest of the squad was trying to suppress the enemy. Sgt. Kent crawled behind a tree but was still about twenty yards ahead of the group in the direction of the gun shots.

Lieutenant (LT) Jefferson ordered the rest of the platoon to move forward and cover first squad. He then radioed back to Headquarters (HQ) and informed them of their current situation communications were spotty as the mountain terrain interfered with the signal.

Sgt. Kent was trying to do his own field dressing and return fire at the same time. While the rest of the squad began to zero in on how many enemy combatants and their exact location. Spc. Dahl, who was next man up looked to see who was closest to Sgt. Kent, his eyes fell on Johnny and he yelled out **"Lang, move up and assist Kent."** Without hesitation Johnny stood up and began to rush to towards Sgt. Kent the rest of the squad suppressed the enemy as he moved forward. As he approached Sgt. Kent's position, an enemy soldier began to charge him firing wildly at his direction. Johnny slid to a knee raised his weapon and pulled the trigger. Three rounds tore through the Taliban fighter chest dropping him to the ground. The adrenalin held off the shock as Johnny began to assist Sgt. Kent with his field dressing while Sgt. Kent laid down cover fire.

The rest of the platoon arrived at their location and Spc. Dahl called out the position of the enemy and the remaining platoon effectively suppressed the enemy and downed two more before forcing them to brake contact and leave the area. The medic ran up to Johnny's position and took over care for Sgt. Kent and told Johnny to get back in the fight.

LT. Jefferson radioed HQ again and updated their status and requested a medivac for his soldier. A few minutes later a radio call came as two Apache gunship helicopters entered the area to provide air support from the initial radio call of enemy contact.

The Apaches were on a routine patrol in the sky's when they heard an infantry units radio call that they made enemy contact but didn't know size of opposition. They radioed back to their command and received permission to deviate from the area and provide assistance. When they arrived, they were updated about the situation and decided to do a fly over of the village and the surrounding area to do an aerial recon to see if they could locate any other possible threats. A few minutes later they radioed back informing LT. Jefferson that there was a mass of possible hostile fighters forming on the edge of the town in the direction that they would be coming from.

After updating HQ LT. Jefferson ordered his unit to fall back and head to the exfil LZ. Once they arrived, they took up defensive position and waited for the helicopter to arrive. A few moments go by and the thud of the blades from the CH47 helicopter could be heard as it maneuvered up the valley escorted by another Apache.

Once back, the unit was debriefed and released for the evening. Billy met up with Johnny who was now calming his mind down and going over what happened. Billy started asking Johnny questions about what went down and everything that happened, Johnny was still distracted by his thoughts.

Johnny snapped out of it after five minutes or so and recounted everything to Billy. After he finished Billy asked if he was ok or if he needed to talk more, but Johnny insisted that he was fine and all he needed was some chow and sleep.

CHAPTER 18

FORGED IN FIRE AND BLOOD

A few weeks went by and they engaged in a few more small conflicts with minor injuries. Claire was worried about Johnny every time he went out and would stay up all night when he was on night patrols. She tried to make more time for him when his around, she still affectionately called him her "ground pounder". Johnny loved every minute he had with her and didn't know how he would have gotten this far in this deployment without her. She kept his thoughts off all the negative things that were going on and gave him something to look forward to.

One morning LT. Jefferson called his platoon together and informed them that they would be swapping out with 3rd platoon from their company who was currently in a remote FOB up the valley a few miles from the village where they had their first engagement. He informed them that they would be there for at least a month and to pack accordingly.

Johnny informed Claire who tried to hold back the tears but was unable to do so. Johnny did his best to ease her concerns, but it was a lost battle. It took a good hour or so for her to calm down and she told him he had better write every day, even if he couldn't mail the letters. Johnny agreed and then left to go pack for his new station.

The day came and Johnny and Billy hopped on the Blackhawk which was taking them up the mountain to their new base.

The FOB they would be occupying for the next month was small compared to the village. It was located on the mountain side and provided clear views when the weather was nice of a small town located to the southeast. Hesco barriers surrounded the compound with four tents surrounded by sandbags for bunks, one tent for medical purposes, one shower and latrine tent and two plywood buildings topped with sandbags were used for the command post and supply storage. Three concrete arc bunkers lined the outer area of the tents and were used for protection from indirect fire and two small diesel generators used to supply power. Above the command building a sign read "WELCOME to HIGHLAND" in big bold letters and just under it in smaller writing "The DISNEYLAND of AFGHANISTAN"

Once there, they rummaged through the tents and selected their beds. This was the first time in about a year that they would share the same room again. Details were divvied up and everyone set up their defensive positions. LT. Jefferson called everyone to form up because he had one announcement that he wanted to make before things got too busy. Once everyone formed up Lt. Jefferson called for SSgt. Peters to read the orders as he walked up to Pvt. Lang and ripped his Pvt insignia off his chest and placed the Private First-Class insignia on instead.

The company cheered as SSgt. Peters finished reading Johnny's promotion orders, everyone then lined up to congratulate him and give him a nice little punch to the chest. Billy lined up last so he could have more time to talk and congratulate Johnny for his promotion.

Things fell into a routine and everyone started to become complacent with their duties. Scheduled patrols through the same villages, constant updates back to HQ, schedule resupply drops and the mundane movies that they had all seen multiple times, everything just seemed to blend together.

Twenty-four days into their rotation the Lt. received intel of a suspected hostile attack on FOB's in the region. Along with them there were three other FOB's that lined the valley. Each one was separated by about ten miles and different elevation. The Lt. made sure everyone used extreme caution when performing daily activities and to cancel all remaining patrols until further notice. He didn't want to chance sending his men into an ambush or be attacked without a full force to defend the compound. Word was passed down to all soldiers of the impending attack and guards were doubled as everyone became on edge.

That evening Johnny was scheduled for first shift guard at night and Billy was on the second shift. Each shift was about fours each and required everyone to use night vision goggles or NVG's during the low light conditions to monitor the surrounding area. Johnny's shift went by with no issues as he stood guard along the wall watching for anything unusual. After his shift, he stopped by and visited with Billy for a few minutes who was located on the south facing wall before heading off to bed. The first night was peaceful and everyone felt that maybe the attack had taken place at another FOB along the valley or was just bad intel.

Intel from J-bad still reported that there was an attack floating around with the Taliban but still no hard location or a specific date. That night went the same as the first, with no signs of hostile activity.

Taliban forces had been watching the base for several days taking note of guard position and trying to find weak points for an attack. They had moved fighters into the area under the cover of night and gathered supplies as the leader of the group planned the attack.

In the early morning hours where the light of the sun barely lit the sky, a loud whoosh passed by the camp. The explosion that followed woke everyone that was still asleep as the soldiers on guard sent the warning out that there was indirect fire coming in. Johnny and Billy both jumped from their racks and threw on their armor and proceeded to the designated bunker for cover most of the soldiers were still in PT's or topless in their boxers and body armor.

More explosions began to blanket the mountainside of the camp as they worked their way closer to the camp before finally falling inside the wall. The bunker shook from the shock waves as the explosion worked their way across the compound sending dirt and debris into the air. Everyone was used to the occasional indirect fire, so they didn't put too much thought into it at the time even though this time it seemed to be accurate and sustained. It only took a few minutes for the explosions to stop and the all clear to be sounded.

As they emerged from the bunker small whistling noises and pops began to fill the air when one of the guards yelled **"CONTACT EAST"** everyone rushed to the east side of the camp and took positions along the wall. A small force of Taliban fighters were shooting down from higher up on the mountain side. They never tried to move in closer and just fired wildly down at them. Sgt. Powel who was second squad's leader noted that it appeared to be harassing fire and for everyone to stay behind cover and to not take a stray round. The Lt. called back to the main base and informed them of the current situation and was informed that they were one of two camps to report such incidents.

Suddenly a smoke trail streaks across the sky from the northwest followed by the guard yelling **"RPG, WEST."** Sgt. Peters ordered third squad to re-enforce the west wall. Another RPG smacked into the wall sending a small dust cloud up into the air. Billy mounted on the west wall about ten yards from the guard post and began scanning the area for the RPG shooter.

Johnny still monitoring the east wall noted that the fire from the east seemed to have lightened. Spc. Rodgers peeked up and called out that more fighters were amassing from the east. Spc. Dahl organized his squad and set up their field of fire to increase the effectiveness in case they did attack from the east. SSgt. Peters had second squad gather ammo for everyone on the wall and sent fourth squad to the command bunker to be held in reserve so the enemy could not gather the true numbers they had available. The Lt. was requesting air support and re-enforcements from Main HQ. Air support would take about twenty minutes and the helicopter designated for re-supply/re-enforcements was currently experiencing engine trouble and no ETA was available.

More Taliban soldiers formed from the west and both groups began firing on the base. Everyone ducked behind the wall for cover and sporadically popped up to return fire. Mortar rounds began falling back down onto the base sending shrapnel and debris flying all over.

Muffled by the explosion a voice could be heard calling out **"Help, Medic…MEDIC."** A soldier from second squad had been hit with shrapnel as he was taking extra ammo for the machine gunners on the west wall. The medic ran out and treated the soldier and called for assistance before moving him into the bunker. The fighters from the east used the chaos of the explosions to move closer to the camp as did the fighters from the west. Spc. Dahl popped his head up and saw the fighters moving in and ordered his squad to open fire.

Johnny popped up and fired a couple of rounds at the group before dropping back behind cover, other soldiers did the same trying to suppress the attack and repel the wave of enemy combatants Spc. Dahl used this time to try and get a good figure on the size of the force from the east.

The soldiers on the west wall had begun returning fire as well and giving updates back to the camp HQ building. *"Lt. roughly 80-100 fighters. Mostly small arms and RPG's. The fighters are pushing in from the west. Over"* the radio buzzed. The Lt. relayed all information back to the main unit while also coordinating with SSgt. Peters and sending orders out to the men.

Billy was returning fire when another RPG screamed through the air hitting the guard post sending the soldier inside flying out and onto the ground. The soldier closest to them ran up to check on them but shook his head and returned to the wall and continued returning fire.

The indirect fire stopped once the Taliban fighters were close to the camp and the rifle fire was becoming more placed then scattered as they were trying to focus the efforts to create an opening to try and breach the wall.

Johnny figured there were about 50-60 fighters from the east that were closing in. Johnny returned fire dropping one of the fighters, then wounded another, the rest of the squad was doing their part as the enemy's numbers dropped down. SSgt. Peters pulled Johnny and another soldier from the east and sent them to the west wall and then had Second squad form up on the east. The rest of first squad was pulled back to rest and continue ammo runs to the wall for the machine gunners and other soldiers that were running low. Fourth squad was eager to get into the fight but were still held back. The enemy was now close enough on both sides to start throwing grenades over the wall.

Johnny took position next to Billy and began firing on the enemy's position. SSgt. Peters went back into the command building and asked, "how long until air support arrives" The Lt. informed him that they were still at least ten minutes out from their location.

The first grenade that came over the wall blew up harmlessly in the open, the second grenade flew over Billy and Johnny's position and hit the ground just in front of Pvt. Cunnings who was bringing ammo to their location, when the grenade exploded sending his body in the air.

Johnny watched as Pvt. Cunnings laid lifeless on the ground as anger filled his eyes. Billy turned immediately and began firing on the enemy wounding one and sending another diving behind cover. Johnny turned around a second later firing wildly into the enemy's location. He pulled out a grenade off of his armor and threw it, hoping to take out another fighter or two. Billy followed suit after Johnny's grenade exploded and tried to place his in the area that the fighter that took cover was at.

The enemy fighters were moving from large rock to large rocks and using washout gulley's as cover as they moved in closer.

Back on the east wall the enemy combatants now reduced to about half their force began to break contact and fall back.

The west wall was still under heavy fire as the enemy fighters pushed their way closer. SSgt. Peters ordered second squad to reinforce the west wall and left only the original security detail on the east wall to return fire as the enemy retreated and to monitor for any signs of another attack. SSgt. Peters then pulled third squad from the wall and replaced them with first squad. He did pull Johnny and the other soldier from first squad off the wall with third squad. Fourth squad was now detailed to help reload empty magazines for the remaining soldiers on the wall.

Inside the command tent the Lt. continued on the radio trying to get updates on re-enforcement and updating main HQ on the ongoing situation. Command informed the Lt. that the inbound attack helicopters that were on their way started to receive ground fire and had to divert to take care of the enemy forces so the re-supply/re-enforcement helicopters could fly safely up the valley to their position. The next closes air support was an AC130 gunship currently refueling in air and 30 minutes out.

Suddenly the fire from the west wall ceased and all fell quiet. Sgt. Peters didn't like that they suddenly stopped but wasn't going to let the opportunity to reorganize and finish redistributing ammo.

The Lt. was informed that re-enforcements were ready for departure, but they were waiting for air support before flying up the valley. The two-attack aircraft had inflicted heavy casualties to the enemy and had to return to base (RTB) and refuel before escorting the other aircraft up the valley. ETA was 40 min for them to arrive.

During the cease fire second squad delivered water and ammo to the guys on the wall and moved other supplies to surrounding area for quicker delivery. Johnny took a small break and sat on a chair just inside his tent.

Even though the air was cold, the adrenalin running through his veins had him sweating. Snow was patchy all over the mountain as the sun would melt a little each day and the slight wind whistled past the tent.

Billy joined Johnny for a few minutes and telling him "Man. This is some crazy shit." Johnny nodded and said "Yeah, you would think that by now they would know not to fuck with us." Billy lifted his head up and asked, "Do you think this is the friendly exchange of cultural idea's that the recruiter told us about." They both laughed and got back up and rejoined the rest. SSgt. Peters pulled guards from the north and south wall to help cover the east and west. The remaining guards had larger areas to cover but would be supported by fourth squad if needed.

The quiet was broken by the sound of a dirt bike or motorcycle of some sort as it came roaring up the path toward the front entrance of the camp located on the east wall. The guard along the wall shouted to the rest that a vehicle was approaching rapidly. SSgt. Peters ran to the wall and waved for the driver to stop. The driver kept coming with no intention of slowing down. SSgt. Peters tried one more time to get the driver to stop but was unsuccessful. He ordered his men to open fire, the motorcycle fell over about 50 yards from the entrance and the driver began squirming on the ground.

A large explosion filled the air as the driver detonated an explosive device that he was carrying on the motorcycle. Everyone in the compound ducked down as debris fell from the sky. Then small arms fire erupted from outside the west wall as the Taliban began the attack again.

Lt. radioed and updated to HQ and received a bit of good news. A small artillery base turned their guns so they could cover the FOB with indirect fire. The Lt. called SSgt. Peters into the bunker and had him relay coordinates to the artillery base. The mountain side to the west lit up with explosions forcing the Taliban into cover again. A guard from the east called out for support as the enemy had reformed and been re-enforced and now on the attack again.

SSgt. Peters ordered fourth squad to support the east wall and redirected the artillery fire to the east. Fourth squad led by Sgt. Enriquez rushed to the wall happy to be joining the fight and opened fire on the enemy forces. Once the last round hit on the west side and the Taliban realized it, they were up shooting and moving again. SSgt. Peters would go back and forth with artillery from west to east and back again keeping the enemy at bay and slowing their advance. One round landed right on an enemy's fighters position causing body parts to fly through the air causing one piece to land near Rodgers. He picked up the severed hand and held it out and asked loudly **"Hey, Any BODY need a HAND."** A collective "Shut the fuck up, Carl." Rang across the unit as snickers of laughter followed closely behind.

The sun was now peaking over the mountain and the artillery unit was now out of shells and was waiting resupply. Another hundred Taliban fighters were getting ready to join the fight amassing just over the ridge line. The fighters from the west had been reduced to about 60 fighters and the east fighters after being re-enforced were now at about 80 strong. Ammo was becoming low and the Lt. wasn't sure how much longer they would be able to hold their position.

When finally, a call on the radio came through that gave the Lt. a great deal of relief. "FOB Highland, this is Puff23" The AC130 was now overhead and ready to assist. Along the west wall the soldiers were engaged in heavy fighting. Johnny and Billy had rejoined the wall and were caught up in the battle when suddenly out of nowhere a storm of hot lead poured down like a hail in a tornado, eviscerating the enemy forces. Pvt. Lance who was next to Johnny and Billy stood up and cheered for the support. Johnny was yelling for him to get down when one of the fighters that was still alive fired and put the round through his chest. Johnny and Billy rushed to his side and began treating his wound and calling for the medic.

Blood was gushing from his chest and Pvt. Lance was having trouble breathing, the medic arrived and asked them to stay and help while he tried to treat his wound. It didn't take long before he started to convulse and then become still. The medic threw the bandages and clotting material down and said a few unsavory words before looking at Johnny and Billy and shook his head. He got up and told them to move his body to the med tent with the other two.

It didn't take long for the AC130 to take care of all the attackers and the re-enforcements that were preparing just over the ridge. Everyone rejoiced that for the time being the battle was over and began to regroup and do a combat assessment of their equipment, ammo and casualties, also known as an ACE report.

A few minutes later the thud of the helicopters could be heard working up the valley as the re-supply and re-enforcements were now arriving. They downloaded the gear and welcomed the new guys to the camp before loading up three wounded and three soldiers killed in action.

The next few days went by smoothly as they cleaned up the base and collected the Taliban bodies placing them in a mass grave site. Soon the main replacements were in bound and Johnny and Billy were back at J-bad where things were a little calmer.

Claire was extremely happy to see Johnny again that she decided to pretend to be sick so she could spend the day with him, hunting for private areas for them to escape reality.

CHAPTER 19

THE LAND OF MILK AND HONEY

The rest of the deployment went by pretty fast after the day of the attack. They went on more patrols and had a few more engagements, but nothing on the scale of that day. Billy and Johnny found a new type of brotherhood that bonded them together. Something that can't be found anywhere but in the heat of battle among fellow soldiers that shared the experience with you.

Each one went on their rest and relaxation trip or R&R just after the halfway point. Billy went first and visited Dean, Trish and Lilly for a few days out of the 15 he was allowed to take. The rest of the time he spent with Britt between Athens and Savannah Ga. Johnny and Claire were able to take their R&R at the same time and decided to go somewhere tropical for a few days before going off to visit family for a few days independently before returning. When at home both the boys tried to avoid the subject of their deployment with their family's as they just wanted to take their minds off of everything on that side of the world. Things did seem to move faster after they returned to Afghanistan.

After being away from the states for 10 months with the exception of their R&R, Johnny and Billy found that the things they took for granted back home were more precious than most people realized. They began making plans for all the things they were gonna do when they got back. Go to the beach, climb a mountain not wearing 60lbs of gear, visit home, buy a fast car, and enjoy the smaller things that life had to offer. Johnny was also planning what he was going to do with Claire, like finding a place for them to live together and taking a real honeymoon. Billy was excited about seeing Britt again since she would be off for summer semester.

One thing they both looked forward to, was real food. The food while deployed wasn't that bad but it was the same week after week. The menu never changed except for the holiday time.

The last two months went by quickly and Billy and Johnny were happy to be heading home in one week. Claire left a day before them to head home and would be waiting for him when he arrived. Dean, Trish and Lilly made the trip back out to welcome the boy's home as well.

When they arrived, the entire regiment formed up and marched to the parade field where all the family and friends were waiting. The commander gave a speech detailing the achievements of the unit in the fight against terror and talked of how proud he was to have served with every one of them.

He finished his speech, called the regiment to attention then released them for the day. It didn't take Billy long to find Britt in the crowd of loved ones and to point out Dean and Trish to Johnny. Claire was with them having found them before the unit arrived. Trish grabbed her boy and hugged him as tight as she could as tears flowed from her eyes. Dean held Lilly and patted his son on the back on the only open area he could find between his wife's arms and told him how proud he was of him. Dean then turned and gave Billy a hug as well and told him "Your father says he is proud of you, and happy you're home." Billy hugged Dean again before giving his attention back to Britt without acknowledging his fathers' remarks. The hug went on for a little longer than Johnny would have liked but would never say anything to his mom about it.

She finally let go of her grip and off they went together as a family. Dean took them all out to eat that night at the restaurant of their choice. They chose a steakhouse that they had frequented before their deployment, hoping it wasn't too busy. The thought of a big juicy steak with a loaded baked potato and fried okra had their mouths watering.

That night at dinner everyone talked and enjoyed the company of each other and shared fun memories of their experiences. Billy recounted a story about duct taping one of their friends to his bunk and putting him outside of their sleeping hooch because the snoring became too much to bear. Johnny and Billy stayed out overnight in the same hotel as his parents before reporting the next day for reintegration training.

Dean and the family stayed for a few days since the boys only had half days and ended up getting the morning half for training. Before they had to head back home so Dean could return to work Trish pulled both the boys to the side and told them "Now boys. I am not getting any younger. Yall need to make honest women out of these girls before they wise up." Billy looked at Johnny who in return was looking back at him as laughter busted out and Johnny replied to his mom "Don't worry mom. We got this." She laughed and said, "Well you better." They then rejoined the others before saying their goodbyes.

The rest of that week and the one after were the easiest two weeks they had in the past year. Everything began to fall back in place and life slowly went back to a normal they hadn't had in a long time. Billy rented an extended stay room for Britt who decided to stay for the month before heading back home to prep for fall semester.

Johnny and Claire began looking for an apartment or house to rent since the on base housing was full. They also decided to tell their parents that they were engaged after they had returned home and were planning a late autumn wedding. They planned to take their official honeymoon after that wedding and would go to an island in the Caribbean that they were still trying to decide upon.

Being home the boys were faced with all kinds of choices they hadn't really paid attention before they deployed but now seemed to be more aware of and harder to make. Johnny loved all the choices he had available now, but sometimes found it overwhelming with the shear amount that there was. Billy felt the same and wouldn't trade it for any other way of life. They respected what the country had to offer and felt sorry for the masses that did not understand how good they really had it.

After a few months back home in Colorado word came down that they were scheduled for another deployment next fall to Iraq. The news came a few weeks before Johnny and Claire's wedding.

Claire and Johnny's family made it back out to Colorado for the wedding and again Trish was in tears. Her little boy was now making a nest of his own. Billy was Johnny's best man and few of his squad mates filled in other groomsmen positions. Ebony was Claire's maid of honor and Claire's younger sister was second followed by a few other friends as her bride's maids. The wedding was a small military style wedding at a chapel they found close to the mountains. Snow blanketed the ground even though it was still considered fall providing the best picturesque venue for them.

After the wedding, they went on their honeymoon and enjoyed two weeks of sunshine and nighttime fun in Grenada. Johnny was in heaven when he was with Claire and couldn't picture his life any other way. Claire felt the same and was happy she decided to give this baby-faced ground pounder a shot. They barely left their hotel room and only did so when they needed a break or some food.

The next few months crawled by as the unit started their field rotation for training and prepping for their next deployment. On the plus side Billy turned 21 and was now able to buy alcohol for the guys that couldn't, including Johnny, well for at least a few weeks before Johnny turned 21.

Summer came around again and only a few months remained before their next deployment. The unit received some new personnel and Billy was finally promoted to Private First Class. Spc. Dahl was promoted to Sergeant and the Lieutenant was promoted to Captain and was replaced by a new lieutenant fresh from the academy. Sgt. Kent recovered from his wound and rejoined his unit and was assigned a temporary desk job until they could place him back in one of the platoons.

Life was in its full routine by this point as Johnny and Billy found themselves training the new guys and showing them the ropes. Billy proved to be extremely knowledgeable and when third squad lost two more people who were transferred to other stations, Billy was assigned second to the squad leader as a team leader. Johnny was happy for Billy and offered him to let him buy beer for the both of them to celebrate. Billy laughed and asked "Hey, aren't you supposed to buy me the beer." Johnny replied "Now what kind of friend would I be if I didn't afford you the opportunity to show just how good a leader you can be. Remember lead by example," they both laughed and carried on with their duties and enjoyed the way things were. SSGT. Peters was promoted to Sergeant First Class and retained his position as platoon sergeant.

July was coming to an end when Johnny arrived home to his apartment, when Claire burst from the bedroom and threw her arms and legs around him. Johnny was happy to see such an affectionate hello but was confused as to why. He hugged Claire until she released her grip from him and stood on her own two feet. "What's going on?" he asked. She just stood there smiling and said "A whole lots going" while she rubbed her belly. At first Johnny looked grossed out thinking she had gas or something and said "Oh. I didn't need to know that." She smacked him on the arm and said, "No. stupid" Rubbing her belly again this time motioning down with her head wanting Johnny to follow with his eyes. Johnny looked down and took a second before it him. "No FUCKING WAY?" he asked with surprise in his voice. "YES, FUCKING WAY" she mocked him.

Johnny hugged her again and then pulled out his phone. "What are you doing?" She asked, Johnny responded "Well, I have to tell Billy, and mom and dad." Claire laughed and told him "Oh OK. Don't even worry if I want to tell anybody yet" mockingly. Johnny went to drop his phone and she admitted she was teasing and that she was planning on calling her parents right after she told him.

Billy congratulated the two and told Johnny that they will have to talk about it the next morning at PT. Johnny asked if she knew how far along she was, and she told him it was at least four weeks. Johnny then made the call to his parents and let them know about the pregnancy. This again led his mom to tears but this time for joy over the thought of being a grandma.

Things finally calmed down from the excitement of the news and the doctor gave them the tentative date of April 10 for the birth. Johnny's unit was scheduled for a September deployment which would put him roughly halfway through his tour before the baby would be born. Claire was taken off the deployment list due to her pregnancy, which Johnny liked because that was one less thing that he had to worry about.

August rolled around and the unit was prepping for their deployment getting everything packed and ready to be shipped. Johnny's family made the trip back out to Colorado in September to see the boys off, Dean gave Billy a message from his dad again, this time Billy gave a letter to Dean and asked him to give it to his father.

CHAPTER 20

IRAQ

The boys arrived in Kuwait and stayed for about two weeks to get acclimated to the region before flying into Camp Speicher by C130 where they would call home for the next twelve months. Right off the bat Johnny wished he was back in Afghanistan, the heat and humidity felt as if it was caressing his body everywhere he went. Billy didn't mind the heat to much but could go for cooler weather himself.

Iraq itself was just as hot as Kuwait was, give or take a few degrees. Sand painted the countryside with waves as if it were its own ocean. Closer to the Tigris River, little towns broke up the farmlands and light vegetation that grew along the river. Further up in the northern part of the country was a small mountainous region distorted the horizon Johnny wouldn't necessarily call them mountain's because they didn't compare to the one back in Colorado. Johnny's unit would spend most of their time to the northeast and east part of the country.

The swap out with the outgoing unit was similar to before, with representatives going over trouble areas, patrol routes and local informants as well as a daily convoy out of the wire to get acquainted with the people that they would be working with on a continuous basis.

The transition went by without incident and the engagement report from the previous year was low, so everyone felt that this would have been an easier deployment then their last one was, plus, everyone enjoyed the lack of mountainous terrain in the area they were assigned and were happy to see more flat areas. Billy was happy about the lack of smaller FOB's that required small unit post throughout the year and that the entire unit would stay together as one for the deployment.

Camp Speicher had a small runway for the C130's and helicopters to land and take off from. The infantry guys stayed mostly on the north end of the base and had a large landing pad for helicopters, that they utilized when doing air assaults. Their aviation support unit was out of Germany, 12th Combat Aviation Brigade.

The base had multiple DFAC's as well as gyms and a small convenience store that resembled a normal shoppette that you would find on other military bases not found in Iraq or Afghanistan. The base also used contractors to pull guard duty and relieved the infantry guys of the stress of having to fulfill that requirement. Other units pitched in and helped, leaving the infantry to focus on missions outside the wire as well as guard duty involving locals that worked on the base.

During the day the temperatures were still nearing triple digits even though they were in the beginning of October. However, there was a twenty to thirty-degree difference at night which made it feel as cold as winter.

By mid-October the temperature had dropped some but was still hot as hell. Johnny had gone on 5 convoy patrols without Billy who would be waiting to greet him when he returned and discuss what he saw and how the patrol went. Billy had a few convoys under his belt and a couple of guard details that he had without Johnny who in return did the same and would greet him upon his return and bring lunch to him during his duties. From the outside looking in, one would think that there was a thing between them and all their buddies would even tease them as well as each other about it.

However, growing up together and going through the things they did since they joined had them closely bonded together.

They still had the occasional patrol and convoy together even though they were in separate vehicles and squads. Johnny was now a driver for his Humvee and Billy was a radio operator in his.

During one of their convoy patrols to see a local informant who claimed to have some intel and a buildup of foreign fighters believed to be a part of ISIS were gathering at a small village east toward the border near Iran. Johnny who was in the third Humvee inline caught in the corner of his eye a patch of sand and road debris that didn't fit the surrounding landscape on the side of the road. He hit the brakes and had his radio operator report it to the convoy commander. The first two vehicles were already too close to the object and had to continue forward to gain distance from it. Johnny backed his Humvee up to gain more ground between him and the questionable debris, while the rest of the convoy pulled off into a security position.

They sat there for an hour or so waiting for the Explosive Ordinance Disposal unit (EOD) to arrive and check out the supposed explosive device (IED). A sergeant dressed in a giant gumby looking suit walked up slowly to roadside disturbance and began swiping away sand and gravel. After several minutes another sergeant that was in communication with the guy in the suit walked up to the commander who was now out of his vehicle watching everything and asked him to move all the vehicles back another hundred yards so he could attempt to disarm the now confirmed explosive device.

The commander obliged and the rear part of the convoy moved back as the two other Humvee's that had already passed the IED pulled forward. The two front Humvee's one of which had Billy inside remained vigilant since they were now separated from their main force and were now easy targets for an ambush.

After thirty minutes the EOD guys packed up and gave the all clear. They removed the device and took it out to a remote area to be detonated. Johnny and the rest of the convoy caught up to Billy and continued on to the informant's village.

They gathered the intel and proceeded back to base where they briefed the other intel guys about the informant's information.

Intel said that they were getting reports from other sources as well about a possible buildup of ISIS fighters in the same region near the town of Kalar.

It only took a few days before an air assault was ordered to the town in order to assess and eliminate the building threat. First and second platoons would be split among a few Blackhawks while third and fourth would insert via Chinook. They would insert along the north and north west side of the village while and Charlie company would insert two platoons on the east to watch the Sirwan River that ran beside the village and make sure that any enemy re-enforcements had their hands full before getting into the village.

The village of Kalar had two main roads that traveled through it. One road led north and south and the other came in from the west and dead ended to the other. The river parallels the north and south road on the east end of town. Scattered throughout the city were large patches of dirt and sand that would be used as a landing zone to infill the soldiers as close to the target as they could get without raising to many alarms.

CHAPTER 21

THE ASSAULT

The helicopters were loaded and flying through the night air as the quarter moon barely lit the sand below them. Only a few months in theatre and this would be their first real test of battle in Iraq. The unit Chaplin held a prayer service for anyone who wanted to attend before their mission was set to go off. The Blackhawks peeled off and headed off to their designated LZ's and the Chinook began its descent into theirs.

There was a target group of buildings around a coffee shop that the ISIS fighters were supposed to be occupying a few blocks into town from their insertion point. First and second platoon would form a perimeter around the target group and third and fourth platoon would be the main assault force. The first main building was a hotel surrounded by two smaller shops with living quarters above them. The second main building was the coffee shop and floors above it which was sided by two multi story houses.

The units moved to their position slowly working their way through the village under the dark night sky. The main force was in position and waiting for the word that the perimeter was set and that Charlie company's platoons that they were also in position. No lights could be seen inside the building which could have been good or bad and only time would tell.

All units reported in and ready as the commander gave the order for the main force to move in. Third platoon would take the larger hotel which appeared to be empty and fourth would split up between two three story houses that bordered the hotel. Once the buildings were secured they would move across the street to the coffee shop and the two buildings on either side of it.

Johnny and Billy split up as first and second squad entered the east building and third and fourth went to the west. Johnny was third in line and followed the lead into the building after the door was kicked in. Sweeping left then right he peeled off into a room on the right side of the hall followed by the two guys behind him.

Billy checked the door of his building making sure there were no traps and then kicked the door in as the lead group filed in. Billy took his spot at the end of the line and followed as the group began to splinter into other rooms. The last three inline stacked up at the bottom of the steps and waited for the rest to join them before pushing their way upstairs. Outside of the building a few shots could be heard coming from the hotel.

Johnny's squad cleared the first floor as the second squad worked their way up to the second. Johnny's squad then reformed on them and followed up before moving to the third. Billy was clearing the second floor of the other building when a radio call came in from first platoon that lights were beginning to come on in the building across the street.

Both of the side buildings were empty, fourth platoon was ordered to reform outside and prepare to cross the street.

Inside the hotel third platoon encountered a few combatants but disposed of them quickly without incident and was now forming up in the lobby of the hotel to begin the assault on the coffee shop across the street.

Daylight was now painting the sky as the order was given to move forward. Charlie company reported a vehicle was approaching the city from the south but did not appear to be hostile. Johnny's squad lined up at the door of their next building as gun fire erupted from the coffee shop sending third platoon to scatter for cover.

Billy's squad was in a better position to provide cover fire as they laid into the building giving much needed cover for third platoon to regroup and come up with an attack plan. Two guys took rounds to their body armor but were ok to continue the fight.

Johnny's squad was then ordered to take the building and see if there were any vantage points, to use in order to control the entrances of the coffee shop. When the door was kicked open a grenade hit the door frame as a figure hurried up the stairs. The door kicker yelled grenade as he dove to the side, the first guy on instinct was moving into the door frame when Johnny grabbed him from behind and jerked him back narrowly missing the explosion as it rifled out the open door. Once it was clear the squad moved in searching every room while two guys guarded the stairs. Second squad moved to the second floor and were immediately fired upon. A few exchanges of rounds and second squad was clear to continue on.

Billy's squad threw a few grenades through the windows from the side to suppress the enemy in the coffee shop as third platoon reformed and got ready to attack. The commander ordered Billy's squad brake contact and join fourth squad as they entered their assigned building. Billy's squad was quick, in and out of the building as no sign of hostiles were found.

Third platoon used a volley of bullets followed by grenades as the platoon bounded back to the front of the coffee shop and made their way into the first floor of the coffee shop while the enemy fighters fell back due to the overwhelming power that the US forces brought down around them. Second platoon spotted the enemy exiting the rear and heading into another building across the street. Billy's squad was ordered to reform and assist on first and second squad in their building. Billy and Johnny were back together and ready to assault the next building.

The back door of their building was a double door so the plan was for first and second squad to form up on one side and third and fourth on the other and file out simultaneously covering the section on their designated side as they approached the next building. When the order was given, Billy was the first one out on his side, he peered across the street as an enemy fighter leaned out the window with an RPG. Johnny was coming out the door when Billy yelled **"RPG"** then turned to see Johnny in the doorway. He looked back at the fighter and then back at Johnny who was just now processing the information. Billy forced his legs to push off and tackled Johnny pushing and pulling him to the side as the RPG crashed into the base of the door exploding and sending shrapnel into Billy's right side. The concussion knocked them both out as they landed on the ground.

CHAPTER 22

AFTERMATH

Billy had blood pooling in his pants as the medic quickly moved him behind cover and began cutting his pants off. The blood was coming from all over his left side. His arm had two large gashes and his side was peppered with cuts and punctures. His leg was worse off as chucks of meat and skin were missing. The medic did all he could to keep Billy alive while the Medivac helicopter was inbound.

The medivac unit was already on standby and when the call came in that there were injuries from the gunfight outside the coffee shop they went ahead and dispatched a helicopter to the area. When a second call came about 10 minutes later they dispatched a second aircraft and prepped a third just in case. At that time, they were unaware of the number of casualties and seriousness of said injuries. On the ground the medic was doing his best to treat Billy and Johnny.

Johnny was regaining consciousness and began to worry about Billy since he wasn't anywhere to be seen. Two other soldiers were trying to calm him down as he got up in a frantic state searching for his friend. The battle was still going on across the street and Johnny was worried about Billy and wanted him to know that he was ok so Billy wouldn't worry about him. The other two soldiers were finally able to calm his frantic nonsense and get him to listen to them. They informed him that Billy was wounded but still currently alive. The medic and another guy took him to the medivac bird that had just arrived. They then told him that he needed to go also but he refused. Johnny didn't want to leave until he was sure the assholes that did this were dead. After fighting with the soldiers for a few minutes the medivac couldn't wait any longer and left with Billy.

Billy had two cords from I.V. lines all over him. Billy was concussed and his vision was slightly blurry. The ringing in his ears muffled the sound of the helicopter as he began to move around for a second. He blacked out again during the flight and the next thing he knew he was watching lights pass over him as he felt like he was floating. Voices could still be heard as blurred blue figures lined him. He blacked out one more time as the doctors and nurses placed him on the surgery table.

Johnny was held in reserve while another medic checked out his concussion, the medic would not clear him to return to the fight. It didn't take long after that for the fighting to calm down as the shots became farther apart and more men from his unit began to appear around him. Sgt Dahl walked up to Johnny and asked if he was ok, in which Johnny nodded and mumbled that he had a severe headache. Sgt. Dahl then said "Well hopefully this will help your head out. We got the sonofabitch that shot the RPG." Johnny gave a thumbs up as his head began to pound. Johnny blacked out from his concussion and as a safety precaution was medivacked to Balad Airbase where Billy was taken to.

The surgeons spent hours doing everything they could, but Billy's leg was too far gone below the knee to save. They were able to save his life and his arm thanks to the medic's quick actions at the battle site along with theirs in assessing the amount of damage. Billy woke up on a hospital bed with Johnny sitting by his side. "Hey Johnny, what happened?" Billy asked. Johnny sat there still in his gear from the assault trying to find the words to tell his friend what happened. "You got injured from an RPG." Johnny said. Billy tried to get up but found it hard and unable to. Billy asked, "Are you ok?" Johnny nodded and continued "They are going to send you to Ramstein Airbase in Germany for more procedures before sending you back stateside." Billy was confused and wondered how messed up he was to be medevacked out of country. Billy could barely move his head down to see his wounds asked Johnny "How bad is it?" Johnny was fighting back some tears told him "Billy, you lost one of your legs and your arm is really fucked up. The doctors don't know if you will have permanent nerve damage or to what extent it will affect you" Billy tried to look but was unable to and was growing worried.

The doc came in and asked Johnny to leave so they could check on the sutures and discuss the upcoming events with Billy. Johnny nodded and told Billy that he would try to come by again before they sent him back to Speicher.

Johnny arrived at the hospital on Balad Airbase where they hooked him up to some machines to monitor his heart rate and blood pressure as well as brain wave activity. Johnny was going to be kept overnight for observation and would return to his unit the next day. They did schedule a cat scan just to ensure there was no further damage to the brain area. When Johnny regained consciousness later that afternoon he talked to one of the nurses to find out where he was. When they informed him of his location he asked if another soldier from his unit was there as well. The nurse told that another soldier did arrive a short time before he did. Johnny talked the nurse into giving him Billy's room information and made his way down the hall. After Johnny saw Billy he made his way back to his room and began to cry. The nurse came rushing in to see if he was ok as he sat on the floor in tears.

The next day Johnny made his way to Billy's bed and talked to him for a few minutes before they sent him off to prep for the flight they talked for a few minutes before it was time to go. Johnny left the hospital and went to transport building and waited for the helicopter that would take him back to Speicher.

A few days went by and Billy was in Germany and had two more procedures to remove the rest of the shrapnel from his body before being flown back to Walter Reed Army hospital for recovery and rehabilitation.

Johnny was in the midst of his deployment and thinking of Billy everyday he was outside the wire as well as his wife and child. During this time Johnny found it harder to focus fully on the mission without his brother there with him.

Johnny would talk to Claire on the phone as often as he could and more so now needing someone to talk to. He would check on her and the baby and tried to get her to give him more information on it. Claire had decided to keep the sex of the baby a secret until he came home for vacation because she wanted to see the look on his face when she told him.

April was approaching fast and the baby would soon be there, and Johnny was on his way home for rest and relaxation. Billy had completed recovery and his first part of rehab and was transferred the VA hospital in Atlanta after he was medically discharged to continue his rehab.

Billy had been home for over a month and was finding life to be harder than he originally thought it would be in his condition. He began to drink to dull the pain and developed an addiction to the pain pills. Britt would come every chance she could to visit Billy and support him in his rehab.

Billy was staying in an apartment not far from the hospital and would normally take a shuttle to and from his appointments. Billy's addiction was beginning to catch up to him and one night at the end of March he found himself about to hit rock bottom.

Britt made the trip from Athens to Atlanta after class on Friday arriving around mid-evening. Billy had just finished a 5th of jack and a couple of pills as he laid in the floor staring at the ceiling contemplating everything. He was wiggling his nub of a leg, laughing and talking to himself "Ha. Ha. I can still feel it." His place was a mess as he had given up on trying to keep it clean or himself even. Dirty to go food containers and old clothes were strewn all over and bottles filled with piss were stacked near the door. Billy hadn't shaven in days and his hair was now greasy mess. Stains peppered the carpet and a foul odor saturated the air.

Britt walked in to find him a disgusting mess, unshaven and unbathed, from the smell had to be about two weeks. Britt became scared for Billy and his condition and tried to get Billy to talk to her and tell her what was wrong so she could help. Billy on the other hand didn't want to talk and did his best to push her away.

Britt would ask him simple questions just trying to get him to open up, but he would just ignore it or tell her he wasn't discussing it. She thought that she would try to clean up a bit while he either sobers up or passes out since he didn't want to talk. As she started to clean, he watched through his now hazy vision and wondered what she was doing. He asked "Hey, hey. What are you doing with all that stuff." Britt responded, "I am trying to clean this place up so it's not so messy or dirty." This angered Billy as he responded "Don't touch my stuff. Who do you think you are. You're not my mother so stop it." Britt became a little emotional but responded in an agitated tone "I may not be your mother, but it doesn't mean I don't love you. I am only trying to help you out." Billy was even more upset, and his words would sting deeply in Britt as he said "LOVE me. LOOK AT ME. I have a STUMP FOR A LEG and my arm is… well look at it." Billy holds out his arm revealing the two deep scars that marked his arm as he continued "You don't love me. You just pity me. The first chance you get, you will leave and that will be all there is." Britt was now in tears as she responded "How can you say that Billy. I have been nothing but supportive of you and tried to help every chance I can. If I wanted to go, I would have left already but no. I keep coming back to help you because I love you." Billy wasn't hearing it as he continued to berate her for touching his stuff and only pitying him.

Britt finally had enough and left crying while Billy crawled across the floor and dumped everything she had put in the trash back out. Billy then passed out there on the floor covered in trash.

Britt was sitting in her car in tears when she decided to make one call as she began her drive back to Athens.

The next day Billy was awakened by a loud knock at the door. Still groggy he sat up and crawled his way to an almost empty bottle of alcohol and yelled for the person to enter.

Sam walked in and almost gagged from the smell, he looked around the room to find Billy sitting near the entrance to the kitchen. Billy looked up but the sleep in his eyes still blurred his vision a little bit. Sam finally spoke "Billy, what are you doing?" Billy immediately recognized the voice and said "What the fuck do you want? I thought I told you I didn't want to see you again." Sam walked over and as Billy went to take a swig from the bottle, Sam grabbed it and ripped it out of his hands and threw it across the room. Billy became extremely angry and yelled "NOW WHY THE FUCK DID YOU DO THAT.?" Sam turned back to Billy and said, "Who do you think you are?" Billy laughed and said, "Your son." Sam bent down and said, "No. My son isn't a weak pathetic boy like you are." Billy replied, "How would you know." Sam wasn't going to let Billy defeat himself and continued to speak, "Oh, I know my son. Because whenever things were hard, he would overcome them. Just like now, he wouldn't let this stop him. He would fight this and beat it." Billy interrupted "You don't know shit. You didn't want anything to do with me or at least not after mom died. You ain't my father and if I could stand up, I would kick your ass." Sam took the challenge and grabbed Billy under his armpits and raised him up. Billy asked, "What the HELL are you doing?" Sam responded "You want to kick my ass? Well I am gonna stand you up so you can." Billy scoffed and replied, "Oh yeah pick on the guy with one leg." Sam then said "Fine I will make it fair and I will stan on one leg also" as he raises his left leg.

Billy was not amused and asked, "Why are you really here?" Sam put his leg back down held Billy steady and said, "Because I received a phone call that some asshole who lived here was skipping his rehab and wallowing in his own self-pity and being a verbally abusive asshole to the girl that loves him" Billy didn't respond to the statement and looked around before asking "Why don't you just leave me alone and go back to your whore." Sam was about to say something in defense of the woman he was with but decided that he would wait until Billy was in a better condition. Instead Sam said "I will leave you alone when I am damn good and ready" as he bent down and picked Billy up and threw him over his shoulder. Billy protested but was still to hung over to put up much of a struggle. Sam took him to the bathroom and turned on the water and tossed Billy in the tub.

Billy squirmed as the cold water shocked him, at first as he begged for his dad to turn on the heat. Sam sat there and watched as he thrashed about and told him that he can have a warm shower when he grows up and stops acting like baby. Sam then made Billy strip in protest and then squirted body wash all over him and told him to make sure he got everything cleaned. The water almost turned black from the filth as he bathed himself. Once done Sam threw him a towel to dry off and went on with cleaning up the apartment.

Billy wasn't going to like the next few weeks. His dad told him that he wasn't going to sit back and watch his son turn into him. Whether or not Billy wanted it, Sam was going to help him and make sure that he started back on his appointments. Billy didn't like it at all and told his father that no matter what he did he couldn't make up for everything he had already done.

Sam started forcing Billy back to Rehab for his amputation and start rehab for his addiction. Billy wouldn't talk to his dad about anything other than his schedule and to tell him when he was hungry. Sam was a little bothered by it but was bound and determined to not give up.

At one of his AA meetings the counselor brought in a friend of his who was the VA hospitals resident Chaplin. He passed out his card to all the attendees that were veterans and then parted ways with the group.

CHAPTER 23

COMING HOME

April was warming up and Johnny made it home just in time to see the birth of his baby. On his first day back Claire finally revealed that they were having a boy. Johnny jumped with excitement and called everyone he could and even e-mailed his other buddies back in Iraq.

Johnny decided to name his son after his grandfather Benjamin and his best friend William (Billy). Johnny was home for fifteen days total and after the birth he only had 8 days remaining. On one day he tried calling up Billy to see what he was doing and to introduce him to his nephew when they flew to Georgia for a few days but received no answer. Johnny called Britt and asked her about Billy, but she wasn't in the mood to talk and told him to call his father.

Johnny called Sam after getting the number from his dad and talked to him for a few minutes and getting informed that Billy had some setbacks and wasn't able to see anybody at that time. Johnny was saddened that he wasn't able to see Billy but was understanding and knew that he was probably still adjusting to everything.

Johnny spent the next eight days with his wife and son and the rest of his family. Things were great until the day came for him to fly back and finish his deployment. This was hard for Johnny to do since he wanted to spend as much time with his family and his son as he could. Knowing he still had a few months to go when he got back just made him a little more depressed.

September was still a good way out and Johnny was already counting down the days until he could get back home again.

Johnny found another soldier to chill with since Billy wasn't there and also worked his way up to be the squad's number two guy, around June, Johnny was promoted to Corporal. The day after his promotion he was out in a convoy in one of the trail vehicles when an IED went off disabling the number two vehicle. The convoy quickly took defensive posture as the medic and two guards went to check on the people inside. The two on the driver side were killed and the other two sustained several injuries. They were medevacked out of the area and the convoy carried on.

June was gone and the boiling hot summer heat was beating everyone down as they all dreaded every daytime operation. Johnny received a letter from Billy telling him about all the rehab and how hard things were for him at first, but things were getting better with the help of his dad. Johnny wrote back telling Billy that if he needed anything to just ask and he would do what he could.

When August finally arrived, things had quieted down again and preparations for returning home were getting underway. Soon the new unit would be arriving, and they would be leaving. The countdown was getting closer as the days ticked off the calendar. The new unit arrived and the transition went smoothly.

Johnny was on the first bird to leave and head home, arriving three days later after it departed from Balad Airbase. Johnny's wife and son were there to greet him along with his mom, dad and sister. Billy also showed with his dad and a prosthetic leg. They all rejoiced with Johnny coming home and were happy that he was safe and sound again.

They all went out to eat and celebrate laughing and joking about all the fun things that they did throughout the whole year. Lilly was full of questions about what Johnny did and how it was over there and also where the baby came from since Johnny was gone for so long. Trish quickly interjected before anyone else could respond. Johnny and Claire shared a laugh at the question before moving the subject on to something else.

Johnny started his re-integration training the next day as the routine from the first time followed. Sam and Billy had to head back early so he could go to physical rehab appointment the following day and Dean and the rest took off a few days later and told Johnny that they would see him in a week or so when he came home for vacation again.

Claire and Benjamin (Benji) enjoyed having Johnny back at home. The baby now able to see clearly smiled every time he saw Johnny and would giggle and laugh at all the faces Johnny made.

Johnny was coming close to the end of his first enlistment contract and wasn't sure what to do. He liked being in the Army and the benefits that came with it, however he thought about spending more time at home with his family. He still had a couple months to think it over and discuss it with them and tried to figure out what would be best.

After completing re-integration training Johnny worked a few half days in Colorado before taking leave for another 15 days at home.

Johnny was welcomed once again by his mom, dad and sister when they arrived at his parent's house and enjoyed a wonderful family meal that Johnny's mom had prepared. Johnny and Claire were given his old room to sleep in and a crib was placed there for the baby as well.

The first day home, they mostly sat around the house and talked, not really feeling like going anywhere or doing anything. On Sunday they went to church and then out to a big breakfast then back home and watched football. Johnny was still getting used to home life again and trying to get out of the mindset of being deployed.

The first Monday Johnny had talked to Billy and planned to hang together for a little while with Claire and his son. On the drive over Johnny happened to catch a bag of trash out of the corner of his eye and slammed on the breaks in the middle of the road. Luckily no one was behind them as Claire reaching for the dash asked what was wrong, Johnny shook it off as a flash back and said he was fine and continued driving. Once they arrived at Billy's apartment they walked in and were greeted by Billy who offered them some snacks. They obliged and all sat around the living room and talked while little Benji was passed around for Billy to see and hold. Johnny noticed Billy's arms and asked how he was, and Billy told him that his arm was good only some spots of nerve damage but not too much. He then told them that he only had a few scars on his side that didn't bother him and that his leg was the biggest thing for him to get over.

Johnny then asked about Britt and Billy filled him in on everything that happened and how he was scared to reach out to her because he was afraid of her rejecting him. Johnny told him that he should at least attempt it, just have closure.

After a few hours Johnny and his family had to go and get back south, Johnny hugged his friend and told him that he would see him again and walked out to the car and drove back home.

The next day Johnny was wanting a chicken sandwich and offered to get some for Claire since the baby was being fussy and everyone else was at school or work. Claire was grateful and told him to surprise her with whatever from wherever he went. Johnny returned almost an hour later and apologized for the delay, that traffic was a little hectic. Claire sat and ate her food with a little peace and quiet as the baby had fallen asleep for his nap. While Johnny watched the baby and carried on small conversation with his wife about what to do with his military contract coming up a few months.

The next two days came and went by in a blur with everyone going on as if it was a normal day.

The following day Johnny took his wife and son around town showing her all the places he went to and, in some cases, what used to be there, and all the things he and Billy did together he took them by the park where he met Billy. Johnny ushered his wife and son out of the car and went to the playground where he held his son while swinging slowly back and forth talking to him on the swing set. Claire took pictures with her phone to cherish the memories they were making. After a while they went back to his parent's house where Johnny told her to go ahead and take the baby in, he was going to make a phone call and then be in shortly. Trish was already starting dinner and Dean had just got home right before they did. Lilly was practicing her writing upstairs and Claire was getting ready to feed little Benji.

CHAPTER 24

THE NOTE

A loud shot rang out and everyone in the house took cover on the floor. Dean looked around and asked where Johnny was, and Claire told him that he was on the phone in the car. Dean told everyone to stay where they were, and he made his way to the door.

The police were there processing the scene, the lead detective walked over to the family who were in a devastated state and turned over the note they had found in Johnny's hand. It read:

Dear Claire and Benjamin.

I love you both with everything I have and it saddens me that I must leave you this way, both of you are the world to me and I want yall to live long and happy lives and not to mourn over me.

To my Mom, Dad and sister,

I love each and every one of you and hope that you and Claire can forgive me for what I have done. I know that this will cause you pain but please understand I can see no other way out of my pain.

To Billy,

I know this is not how we pictured our lives' going and that we would always be around for each other and be there no matter what. I want to thank you for everything you have done for me and know that I am deeply sorry I cannot repay you.

Deep inside I have been fighting myself and this was the only way out I could find. Even though it was out of my hands I feel responsible for everything that Billy has been through. If I would have noticed sooner he may not have been beat so much by his father. If I was a better friend maybe he and Maddy would have been together and I wouldn't have caused him the pain of betrayal he felt that day. If I was wiser maybe I could have stopped him finding out about his dad and his girlfriend and not watch as his world turned upside down. Had I been quicker maybe he wouldn't be in the situation that he is in now and all the suffering that is due to it. I feel as if I have let him down and no matter what I do I will never be able to make up for failing him.

I have also failed my wife because even though I love her, the pain from being dumped by Maddy still hurts and I feel as if there is still a part of me that I can't give to Claire because of that and I wanted to be able to give Claire my all. I love my son with everything and regret that I will not be able to be around as he grows and becomes a man himself.

I am haunted in my sleep of the first man I ever killed even though he was trying to kill me. His face is imprinted I fear on my soul and no matter where I am he is there.

I am afraid because I miss the feel of combat when I am at home and thrive to be back. Even though I have everyone around me that I love I feel out of place and alone. As if this is all a dream and I cant wake up. I tried to force myself into not believing this but nothing I do seems to help. I didn't want to burden any one with my demons and did not feel it would be fair to all of you.

I feel a great pain at the friends we lost over there and just tear myself apart knowing that there was more we could have done. I always ask myself why it was them that lost. Why couldn't I have been the one to take the round or the grenade, so they could be at home returning to their loved ones.

I am sorry for everything that I have done, and for all the pain I have caused. To each of you I give my love and I hope that you all understand and forgive me.

To my son, Your life is just beginning and I know you will have a lot of questions when you get older, just know that I love you more than anything and that I will be watching from wherever I go after I have left this place. Be good to your mother and be a stronger man then I was.

With all I am and all I will ever be. Goodbye

The funeral was scheduled for the following Saturday. The police ruled it as a suicide and offered the pistol that Johnny had purchased a few days prior to him taking his life back to his father. Johnny's mother and wife cried for the next three days before the funeral. Billy was informed by Dean and had his dad rush him down.

The family informed his unit of the tragic event, a few of the soldiers that he had gotten to know made their way out to Georgia for all the services. Billy didn't know what to do or think and wondered why Johnny never confided in him and let him help. The only thing he knew to do was call the one girl who was always by his side.

Britt showed up the day before the service started and visited the family and Billy. They talked for a long while before she had to get to her parent's house and get ready for the next day.

Visitation was scheduled for the same day as the funeral and would start at 10 a.m. and conclude at 11 a.m. The funeral service would then start at 12 followed by the procession at 1 p.m. which would then conclude with the burial service.

Johnny's family could not keep their eyes dry as the day went on and the service started. When the preacher asked if anyone wanted to say anything Billy approached the podium and struggled through his speech. He talked about all the things that they did and got into as kids, he told some of their secrets that they kept from everyone else especially Dean and Trish. He just recounted their life together and what he meant to him. Once he finished Johnny's dad stood up and gave his speech before thanking everyone that showed up.

As they walked down the path to his grave site his mother collapsed to the ground not wanting to accept what was happening. Dean picked her up and helped her the rest of the way. Billy and Britt helped Claire with the baby and as she stumbled her way down.

They finally lowered Johnny's body down as taps played in the background and all of them broke down one last time.

CHAPTER 25

JOHNNY

Johnny suffered from depression that developed when he was young. He never understood what it was or that he even had it at first and didn't know how to deal with it. Watching other around him and seeing how they lived their lives; Johnny didn't want to talk about his issues and bring anybody else down. So, he would put on his happy face and do his best to be joyful and full spirited.

The depression didn't run his life all the time. He would have good times when things seemed to be normal and he wasn't downed by any negative thoughts plaguing his head. He took full advantage of these moments by dating and doing things with his friends and family.

Occasionally Johnny would reflect on his depression and try to figure out where it started and how he could fight it.

Johnny's guilt started when Billy's mom died, he felt a pit in his stomach that didn't seem to go away at first as he felt sad for his friend's traumatic experience. The pit moved as Johnny's thoughts changed and eventually started what would end up being a multilayer cloud that would cloud his mind. His thoughts turned to how unfair it was for Billy to grow up without a mom and he did have one.

The next incident came when he found out that Billy's dad was abusing him. He was so excited that his friend was back that he ignored all the signs that there was something wrong and didn't see it sooner. His mind raced thinking that Billy already lost his mom and now his dad was treating him poorly. He couldn't comprehend how Billy could be subjected to this and he had a loving family waiting for him back at home.

Now at this point Johnny wasn't sure what this feeling was or what it would end up being. He only knew that his mind would let it go and he was afraid to say anything because he didn't want people thinking he was weird or something like that.

Years would go by and Johnny mind would always bring those incidents up and he would have to hide his sorrow from his friend.

The third thing that happened and made Johnny realize that maybe there was more going on inside him then he thought before was the day Maddy came to his house when he was alone. The look of betrayal and anger that he saw on Billy's face when he got caught with her just added to the storm that was already there inside his head. It didn't matter that he made up with Billy and things seemed to get back to normal, his mind wouldn't let anything go. Being a teenager, he didn't know why and thought that maybe everyone had things in their head that bothered them and figured if they weren't saying anything then he didn't need to either.

A few years later and Johnny would be hounded by his breakup with Maddy. His first real crush and the one that he had been intimate with first had told him that she didn't want to be with him anymore in a letter while he was away from home. If not for the other things that he had haunting him, then he may have been able to get over it when he found someone new. However, with everything else floating around in his head, it got absorb into the folds of this darkness to linger.

Johnny would find some peaceful days from time to time and even found a new love to help occupy the parts of his mind that weren't covered in the dark cloud that was now bigger than he realized. With Billy and now Claire in his life, his mind became a battlefield as he was growing tired of having these bad thoughts of guilt and betrayal and wanted the good thoughts of the people in his life to be the only thing he thought about.

At first the war in his head seemed to be winnable, things were looking up and he had a good constant in his life. Then came the day of his first encounter with Taliban forces in Afghanistan. Even though his training took over that day and his body and mind seemed to react like a well-oiled machine, the one thing he wasn't trained for was dealing with his action afterwards. The hostile fighter that charged at him had pure unfiltered hate in his eyes and when Johnny fired into him, that face imprinted on his mind. The other battle Johnny was fighting now became questionable of its outcome. Johnny hoped that he wouldn't have to deal with anything like that again and tried to bury it deep down where he hoped it would never resurface.

Johnny battle was far from over and the mind can only take so much. When that battle at FOB Highland came around Johnny was already questioning what he could do to stop these thoughts but nothing seemed to work. His internal battle became even harder when he witnessed two of his comrades fall in the ensuing fight for their FOB. Even though they came out victorious, Johnny felt as if he had lost. He would curse himself in his head "If only I had been more cautious with my shots and ammo then I wouldn't have needed resupply." And "Why did I shout at him to get the fuck down. I could have tackled him and he would still be here." Johnny now felt like the battle in his head was turning and his efforts were now for not.

When he returned home from his first deployment, Johnny thought this was what he needed to get his mind right. Thinking that being back home and having no enemy or chance of battle coming around would help him settle his mind. After a few weeks of this now more peaceful bliss his mind started to wander back to Afghanistan and the adrenalin he had in the midst of the battle and how he now missed it. Johnny didn't know why that was the case and didn't want it to be but thought would not let him push those feelings aside. His mind was starting to feel crowded and he needed to find a way to make room.

When Johnny found out that Claire was pregnant it almost seemed as if his mind was wiped clean. His thought became of only her and the baby and what they were going to do. He finally felt that he would be at peace and that nothing would change it.

Then came his deployment to Iraq. Once it was time to leave for his deployment, the thoughts and feeling he believed were gone now wiggled out of the recesses in which they hid.

From the first incident to the ones that are still left, Johnny always looked happy and in good health on the outside. No one would have ever thought anything bad was going on with in him. Everybody would have jumped up for him at the any sign that he may have been in distressed and would have done all they could to help him. Yet Johnny didn't know what to do or if he should even say anything at all. As time went on and more and more things happened the less he felt like his was part of the group and more alone when it came to his thoughts. He would do anything he could for everyone else if he knew they were going through the same thing and even take away their pain and darkness if he could. Yet, when it came to himself, he was lost and didn't know what or who to turn to.

When the RPG almost killed Billy and himself, Johnny had wished that it did kill him there and that Billy was left unharmed. He would curse himself more, wishing he had reacted quicker and moved faster so Billy wouldn't have had to sacrifice himself for him. Johnny didn't want anyone to have save him but wanted everyone to be able to count on him to save them if needed.

When he saw the after math of the explosion and the condition that Billy was in Johnny blamed himself for everything. Having his best friend, his brother sent back home injured, all but pushed him to the edge of his mind. He felt that there was no more room left for anything else.

Johnny made it through the rest of his deployment and returned home his wife, son and family. However, everything that he had been through returned as well.

When he went on vacation after returning one thing that he didn't expect to push him over the edge or even entertain his thoughts was how life kept going for everyone else. It didn't quite get to him after his first deployment but now it seemed to have been the last thing left for him. The feeling of missing combat and the sights of the dead that floated through his head, the betrayal and the heart break were all there to welcome this newfound alley in their battle for Johnny.

As he watched his family go on with their day to day lives as if nothing had happened and the feeling as if no one seemed to care about him or what he had been through pushed Johnny over the edge. While at home Johnny pinned his note one day while his wife and son took a nap and everyone else was at work or school. He made it a point to say goodbye to his friend and to show his son all the things that he used to enjoy when his was young. He used the excuse to go get lunch one day to be alone and purchase the firearm that he sat his mind one as the means the clear his mind.

Johnny left everything and everyone behind the day his ended his haunts. In doing so, he implanted haunts on all his loved ones. Left to go on with their lives carrying this burden that Johnny was hurting and they were not able to help him. Wondering why he never asked and did they do wrong for him not to come to them with his problems. If only he had spoken up or asked for help. Maybe then he could have found the peace he sought, instead of causing more pain that he feared he would have.

CHAPTER 26

LIFE GOES ON

Claire moved back home with her parents but still flew Benji out to Georgia to visit his grandparents and aunt. After two years had passed, she finally met another person and settled down with him and had two more children. She never stopped loving Johnny and always had a piece of her heart dedicated to him. Claire didn't know how she would tell Benji when he was older about his dad and only knew that it was the hardest thing in the world to think about which she did on certain occasions. The man she married was good to her and treated her and Benji very well. She had told him about what happened, and he was very understanding.

Claire's husband would even fly Benji out himself, after he met Johnny's mom and dad a few times and got to know them. He never tried to take over the role of Johnny when it came to Benji but still treated him like his own son.

Dean and Trish took a little longer to get over the fact that Johnny was gone. They found it even harder whenever Lilly would ask about him and wonder what he was doing. Trish spent many nights after crying herself to sleep as Dean laid there listening knowing there was nothing he could do to help.

They did enjoy every visit they had with their grandson and would take him about the town and even to visit his father's grave and place flowers there. After a few years they were able to find peace within the pain and did their best to keep up with Claire and also Billy as they considered them family and would find joy in hearing the stories they had of Johnny.

A few years passed and Lilly was starting her fifth-grade year of school when a mother of a student a few grades below her came up and asked her how her family was doing and that she was so sad by the news of her brothers passing. Lilly asked her how she knew him, to which she stated that they go all the way back to high school. The lady then asked if she would tell her mom and dad that Maddy said hello and that she was sorry to hear what happened. Lilly nodded and went on about her school day.

Lilly would have her days where she would cry at the thought of her brother and other days where she would brag about how awesome he was. Lilly would eventually grow up and become a businesswoman and ended up marrying a Marine veteran. She found it tough to put up with him from time to time but loved him regardless. Lilly went on to have a few kids of her own and even talked her husband into naming one of their sons Johnny.

Billy finished all of his rehab and even had a few private sessions with the Chaplin and discussed what he was going through. The Chaplin even helped Billy work things out with his father. He was now working as a security advisor for corporation based in Atlanta where he settled down. He made up with Britt after a long apology and many attempts to get her to give him a second chance. She eventually did give him that chance and each day he did all he could to prove that he was in love with her and would do everything within his power to show her that every day they were together. Britt never stopped loving Billy and only wanted to make sure that Billy was truly back to being his old self again.

They both ended up getting married and having three children the first son was named after Johnny and Sam. Then came a daughter who was named after Billy's mom, followed by a second son who Billy asked Dean if it was ok to name him after him. Dean felt honored and told Billy that it was more than thoughtful but didn't have to if he wanted to use another name. Billy assured him that with everything he had been through and how much his family stepped up and helped him, that he was more than positive that he wanted to name his son Dean.

Sam ended up marrying the woman he had been dating and moved closer to Atlanta to be around his son more often. It took some time and several visit to the Chaplin for Billy to finally forgive his father and himself for everything that happened and began to healing process while making up with his father.

Sam took every opportunity to help Billy and ended up becoming a volunteer at the VA hospital and helping other soldiers as well. Sam's new wife Francine was a nurse at a hospital near their hometown but was able to transfer up to a hospital in Atlanta when Sam wanted to move. She finally found some common ground with Billy and developed a relationship with him and Britt and fully took on the role of grandma to their kids.

Life continued for everyone at different paces. The pain they all felt when Johnny took his own life never left them. They would find ways to cope with it as best they could but that was even a day by day process for most part but even on the best days the pain was still there.

END.

Printed in the United States
By Bookmasters